THE AMERICAN EYE

Edward Hopper, *Second Story Sunlight*, 1960. Oil on canvas, 40″ × 50″.

THE AMERICAN EYE

Eleven Artists of the Twentieth Century

JAN GREENBERG AND SANDRA JORDAN

Delacorte Press

To my grandson Benjamin Kaye Avram, with love.
J.G.

To Lindsay Jordan Morgenthaler and Gay Jordan Elwell.
My aunts. Lucky me.
S.J.

Published by Delacorte Press
Bantam Doubleday Dell Publishing Group, Inc.
1540 Broadway
New York, New York 10036

Library of Congress Cataloging-in-Publication Data
Greenberg, Jan.
The American eye: eleven artists of the twentieth century /
Jan Greenberg and Sandra Jordan.
p.   cm.
Includes bibliographical references (p. 116) and index.
ISBN 0-385-32173-2

1. Art, American—Juvenile literature.   2. Art, Modern—20th century—United States—
Juvenile literature.   3. Artists—United States—Biography—Juvenile literature.   4. Art
appreciation—Juvenile literature.   [1. Art, American.   2. Art, Modern—20th century.
3. Artists.   4. Art appreciation.]   I. Jordan, Sandra (Sandra Jane Fairfax)   II. Title.
N6512.G695   1995
709´.2´273—dc20
[B]94-30625   CIP   AC

Manufactured in Italy
October 1995

10 9 8 7 6 5 4 3 2 1

ACKNOWLEDGMENTS

Every effort has been made to contact the original copyright holders of the material included. Credits for the photographs of works of art appear on pages 112 through 114 in the list of artworks.

Page 5, private collection; page 7 (two), courtesy of William Dove; page 16, courtesy of Catherine Kreuger; page 17, Metropolitan Museum of Art; page 26, private collection; pages 35 and 41, courtesy of Thomas H. and Rita P. Benton Testamentary Trusts, VAGA, New York; page 47, courtesy of Earl Davis; pages 52 and 54, courtesy of the estate of Romare Bearden; page 62, © Grand Central Gallery, courtesy of the Isamu Noguchi Foundation; page 65, © Kevin Noble, courtesy of the Isamu Noguchi Foundation; page 69, courtesy of the Isamu Noguchi Foundation; page 72, private collection; page 76, © Dan Budnik 1979, Woodfin Camp and Associates; page 79, Smithsonian Institution; page 86, © Hans Namuth; page 90, The Andy Warhol Museum, Pittsburgh; Founding Collection, Contribution The Andy Warhol Foundation for the Visual Arts, Inc.; page 107, Estate of Eva Hesse, courtesy of Robert Miller Gallery.

This book would not have been possible without the help of many people. We are especially grateful to:

Anita Duquette, Whitney Museum of American Art; Mrs. Noel Oursler of the Edward Hopper House in Nyack, New York; Amy Hau, Isamu Noguchi Foundation; Earl Davis; William Dove; Catherine Kreuger; Henry Adams; Barney and Pam Ebsworth; Tom Armstrong, director of The Andy Warhol Museum; Mary Ann Steiner, director of publications at the St. Louis Art Museum; John Van Doren; Jeanne Greenberg; and George Nicholson, without whose confidence and support we never would have started these art books.

And thank you to Margy Boyd, San Francisco Museum of Contemporary Art; Gregory J. Perrin, estate of Romare Bearden; Diana Bulman, Robert Miller Gallery; Robert Panzer, VAGA; Barbara Cox, National Museum of American Art; Peter Stevens, administrator, Collection of Candida and Rebecca Smith; Stephen Campbell, Thomas H. and Rita P. Benton Testamentary Trusts; Woodfin Camp; and Peter Namuth.

Last but never least, gratitude to the patient, intelligent, and thorough people at Delacorte Press—our editor, Karen Wojtyla; Pearl Young, who keeps things going no matter what is happening around her; the chief copy editor, Barbara Perris; the designer, Susan Clark; Beverly Horowitz; Craig Virden; and all the other people without whom this would be a manuscript and some pictures, not a book.

Stuart Davis in his studio.

"Some of the things that have made me want to paint outside of other paintings are: American wood and ironwork of the past; Civil War and skyscraper architecture; the brilliant color on gasoline stations and chain-store fronts, and taxicabs; the music of Bach; . . . fast travel by train, auto . . . electric signs; the landscape and boats of Gloucester, Mass.; 5 & 10 cent store kitchen utensils; movie and radio; Earl Hines hot piano and Negro jazz music in general, etc. In one way or another the quality of these things plays a role in determining the character of my paintings."

—Stuart Davis

CONTENTS

PREFACE

Each book we write together is a new journey that takes us to unexpected places. This one began when we visited the Isamu Noguchi Garden Museum in Long Island City, where Noguchi worked and lived. We went because we wanted to see many of the sculptor's works in one place. The experience we had there left us stunned and exhilarated, leading to an ongoing conversation about the ways an artist's life and art intertwine.

In our earlier books, *The Painter's Eye* and *The Sculptor's Eye*, we concentrated on living artists we could interview. For *The American Eye,* we focused on artists whose careers could be viewed from beginning to end in order to see how life and art reflect each other and how both could be understood in response to the American experience. There were many artists who paved the way for a new American art. We have chosen eleven who particularly stood out for us.

Woven in and out of their stories are discussions of individual artworks. We talk about these paintings and sculptures by asking some questions using the language of art. What do you see? Identify what is there. All artworks are made up of the elements of color, line, shape, and texture. How are these elements composed? What is the feeling expressed by the artist's use of them?

Working on this project, we have visited many artists' homes, from Jackson Pollock's studio in Springs, Long Island, to Thomas Hart Benton's house in Kansas City. We wanted to see for ourselves what the artists saw, the landscape and the light that inspired them. We hope your encounters with American art, whether in books, museums, sculpture parks, or public places, will be an adventure, a journey leading you in new directions.

1

THE SPIRIT OF THE PLACE

"What do we call 'American' outside of painting? Inventiveness, restlessness, speed, change. Well, then, a painter may put all these qualities in a still life or an abstraction, and be going more native than another who sits quietly copying a skyscraper."
—Arthur Dove

Ever since the colonies declared their independence, most Americans believed that the main business of America was business. These practical, hardworking settlers did not consider the arts—from theater to painting—useful occupations. After all, land needed to be claimed; farmland plowed; churches, bridges, and later railroads and factories built.

Of course, the desire to create, to make something beautiful, is part of being human, so from the time of the earliest people, art existed in America. Sometimes it took the form of beautifying everyday objects such as Native American pots and weavings; later the colonists' quilts and furniture. There were trained artists, too, very successful ones. But the public's attitude both discouraged and infuriated American artists. European art always took first place.

In the early 1900s there was a strong feeling among artists that the United States was long overdue in developing art that did not look to European traditions. Everybody agreed that the heart and soul of the new country should be reflected in its art. But what would this art be like? How would it develop? Opinions differed about that.

Two schools of thought emerged. One looked for inspiration from life in the city, from ordinary people, and from technology and inventions.

The other believed that nature and the spirit of the vast American landscape should shape American art. These themes can be represented by two equally persuasive but quite different figures on the New York art scene—Robert Henri and Alfred Stieglitz.

Born in Cincinnati, Ohio, in 1865, Robert Henri was a well-known painter and an outspoken teacher who insisted that art must reflect an American point of view. Henri's students did not paint the romantic landscapes or portraits of aristocratic-looking men and women that were the subjects of art in the European tradition. He sent his students out into the streets, alleys, saloons, and train yards of New York to paint what they saw. To Henri anything qualified as a subject for art. In *The Art Student* [FIG. 1], his subject is painted against a plain background, her eyes full of earnest human questions. She is shown at the end of a hard working day, her clothes paint-stained and her hair messy, instead of being glamorized as establishment painters would have shown her.

This doesn't sound like a revolutionary idea today, but then it stirred passionate debate. In 1908, with seven equally rebellious artists, Henri put together an independent exhibit. Their group came to be called The Eight, and their exhibit earned them the mocking nickname the Ashcan school because most of them painted realistically gritty scenes from urban life.

FIG. 1 Robert Henri, *The Art Student (Portrait of Miss Josephine Nivison)*, 1906. Oil on canvas, 77 1/4″ × 38 1/2″.

The second opinion-maker was Alfred Stieglitz, a pioneering photographer and guiding spirit behind the exhibition space named the Little Galleries of the Photo-Secession. Known to everyone by the address of its building, 291, it was the only important gallery in New York that showed photography and avant-garde art [FIG. 2]. Stieglitz, born in Hoboken, New Jersey, had studied in Europe. He had discovered that with the invention of the camera amazing changes were taking place in European art. Freed from their role as recorders of events and likenesses—because, after all, the camera could record faster and more accurately—artists, especially painters, began to break new imaginative ground. For example, they could emphasize the elements of painting (texture, color, line, and shape) instead of imitating realistic subject matter. Stieglitz believed in art that did not depend on realism but captured the spiritual essence of life, which resided in nature, not in technology. This, he said, should be the goal of American artists. The gallery 291 became a haven for artists whose convictions matched his own.

FIG. 2 Alfred Stieglitz, *The Street, Winter,* 1903. Gelatin silver print.

On February 17, 1913, in the Armory of the Sixty-ninth Regiment in New York, an exhibit of new art opened that shocked the public. *The New York Times* labeled the Armory Show "pathological." Outraged officials wanted to shut it down "to protect public morality," so naturally 250,000 people paid to get in.

American artists—the art establishment as well as rebels like Robert Henri and other members of the Ashcan school—participated in the show, but the most startling of the 1,600 pieces on view were by European mod-

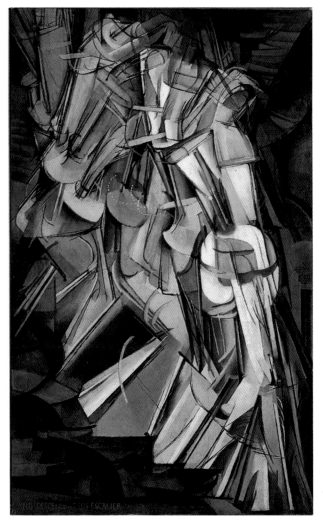

FIG. 3 Marcel Duchamp, *Nude Descending a Staircase, No. 2*, 1912. Oil on canvas, 58″ × 35″.

ernists. One critic called French artist Marcel Duchamp's *Nude Descending a Staircase, No. 2* [FIG. 3] "an explosion in a shingle factory." In this cubist painting the artist divided the subject into blocks of color to show several views on a single canvas. The cubists questioned the conventional aim of painting—to present an illusion of a three-dimensional object on a flat, two-dimensional surface.

Stieglitz had already exhibited some of the European artists in his shows at 291, but he had never attracted big crowds or the attention the Armory Show received. After that show, despite the public jeers, many American artists and patrons who saw the innovative work realized that the time had come for a change. But they didn't want to imitate the Europeans. Within the next few years several of the artists whose work Stieglitz supported—including Arthur Dove and Georgia O'Keeffe—would create their own versions of modernism, based on an American vision.

Progress came slowly, marked by the gradual achievements of these and other highly individual artistic personalities such as Stuart Davis and Thomas Hart Benton. The influence of these early painters continued throughout the thirties and the Great Depression. After World War II came a generation of young American artists born of the depression and nurtured by government programs supporting the arts. The spirit of America was brashly confident. With newfound patriotism, the country celebrated all things "made in the U.S.A.," including American art. The rise of Jackson Pollock and the abstract expressionists heralded a new age. Energetic, inventive, and bold, their art expressed American freedom; New York was proclaimed the center of the art world.

These artists brought geographic and ethnic diversity, and often flamboyant personal philosophies, to their art. Touched by joy and sorrow, each portrayed his or her own experience of America. Edward Hopper, a student of Robert Henri, said, "The man's the work. Something doesn't come out of nothing." The stories of these artists chronicle the story of American art as it unfolded in the twentieth century.

Edward Hopper in Maine.

2

ARTHUR DOVE

1880–1946

AMERICA'S FIRST ABSTRACT PAINTER

Arthur Dove transformed the spirit of the American landscape into gentle, joy-ful paintings. His style was personal, based on emotions, and derived from nature. The artists, including Georgia O'Keeffe, with whom he shared this sensibility were more interested in painting ideas than in presenting realistic subjects. One of America's first modern artists, Dove composed his paintings in a new way by emphasizing color and shape rather than imitating reality.

Arthur Dove was so soft-spoken that his friends nicknamed him "the whispering kid." Yet when he was only twelve, he resigned in protest from his church after it refused to allow an atheist to express his opinion. Clearly this mild-mannered boy had another side. His parents discouraged their son's nonconformist behavior. When he became an artist, they disapproved, and the rest of the world was indifferent. But he believed in himself.

Born in Canandaigua in upstate New York, Dove grew up in the nearby town of Geneva. His father, a successful building contractor, was able to provide his family with all the advantages. Arthur Dove lived in a big white house, took piano lessons, and pitched for his high-school base-ball team.

A local schoolteacher gave him a few private painting lessons, but other than that his exposure to art was limited. However, a middle-aged neighbor, Newton Weatherly, an amateur painter, took Arthur under his wing. Weatherly used to take left-over scraps of canvas and stretch them for Arthur to paint on. The boy roamed the countryside with Weatherly, hunting and fishing in the woods and lakes near the town. These ramblings in the company of an artist sharpened his eye for the details in nature.

Of Weatherly, Dove later wrote, "He was like cloth and vegetables and leaves in the woods." In many ways, Dove modeled his own character on the earthy self-reliant traits he so admired in his older friend. His paintings, too, are rooted in the soil, filled with images of the wild rural landscape of his childhood.

Arthur did so well in school that his father sent him to Cornell University to study law. But his humorous cartoons in the yearbook prompted his art teacher to suggest that he become an illustrator. By Arthur's senior year, he had given up law for art. His conservative father reacted to this decision with predictable fury. Arthur responded equally predictably—he ran off to New York City.

The twentieth century erupt-

Arthur Dove as a teenager in Geneva, New York.

Arthur Dove in Paris.

ed with new ideas, new inventions, new technology, and new possibilities. In the early 1900s the airplane, the automobile, and the wireless telegraph were developed. America emerged as a world power, with New York City as the center of energy. The young man from Geneva had arrived at the right time.

Dove's drawings soon began to appear in popular magazines such as *Harper's* and *The Saturday Evening Post*. He became part of a lively group of artists who also worked as illustrators. Every evening they gathered in saloons where fifty cents bought dinner with wine and they could discuss art and listen to music all night long. With a job and a new life, Dove felt mature and ready to settle down. He married "the girl next door," Florence Dorsey from his hometown.

The couple lived in New York for five years and then decided to move to Europe so that Dove could study painting. In 1908 Paris reigned as the capital of the art world. All serious young artists wanted to go there. America might be the land of opportunity, but Europe remained the center of taste and refinement. Dove returned to New York eighteen months later, convinced he could be successful as a full-time artist. Unfortunately "it was not possible to live by art alone," so he began illustrating again to support his family, especially since his son, William, had been born.

Later that year, Arthur Dove met Alfred Stieglitz. The famous photographer and art dealer understood Dove's work and offered immediate support. They made an odd couple. Stieglitz, an urban Jewish intellectual, educated in Europe, was brilliant but argumentative and domineering. Dove's demeanor seemed gentler; he was a well-mannered young man from a provincial background. However, the two were united by a belief that the established art of Europe, so admired in America, had proved inadequate to express contemporary life.

Joining Stieglitz's gallery also marked a change in Dove's style. Before that he had painted realistically. Now, by reducing objects to patterns of color and shape, he began to eliminate representation in his work. A photograph showed what a scene looked like; Dove tried to show how it felt. Intuition rather than reason guided him. This spiritual approach, based on feelings and inspired by nature, can be seen in one of his first attempts at abstraction, *Abstraction Number 3* [FIG. 4]. Here he simplified the shapes of branches and leaflike forms, using overlapping areas of earth tones. The loosely painted surface, the somber color, and the twisting lines of the tree express the essence or spirit of the landscape, but the image is not a direct illustration. This painting radically departed from the realistic art that was being shown in America at that time.

Unfortunately people didn't understand Dove's new style, and his first one-man show, titled The Ten Commandments, failed commer-

FIG. 4 Arthur G. Dove,
***Abstraction Number 3,* 1910.**
Oil on composition board,
8 3/8″ × 10 1/2″.

cially. In fact, his pastels were so disturbing that some art students in Chicago made effigy dolls of Dove and stuck them with pins. What upset them so much? For one thing, Dove's subjects seemed to dissolve into the background of the paintings.

In *Cow* [FIG. 5] the circular brown-and-white dappled shapes vaguely resemble a cow, but the animal seems to merge into its surroundings. Dove saw life as a state of continuous change and movement. He expressed this by blurring and overlapping his shapes to effect a sense of motion. His idea took hold later in the works of American artists such as Stuart Davis and David Smith. But in 1911, the public rejected it.

Dove needed to support his family, so they moved to Beldon Farm near Westport, Connecticut, where he raised chickens and vegetables.

FIG. 5 Arthur G. Dove, *Cow,* 1911. Pastel on linen, 18" × 20 5/8".

In 1917 the United States entered World War I. During the war, Dove survived by producing eggs, a high-priced commodity. Up before dawn, in bed at midnight, he forced himself to remain cheerful despite the lack of time to paint and the news from New York that gallery 291 would soon close. Americans were too focused on the war to think about modern art. If the public expressed any interest in art at all, they wanted realistic, patriotic paintings. Dove turned to his family for financial support, but his father, who still disliked his painting, refused. "I won't encourage this madness," he told Stieglitz, who tried to put in a good word for his artist.

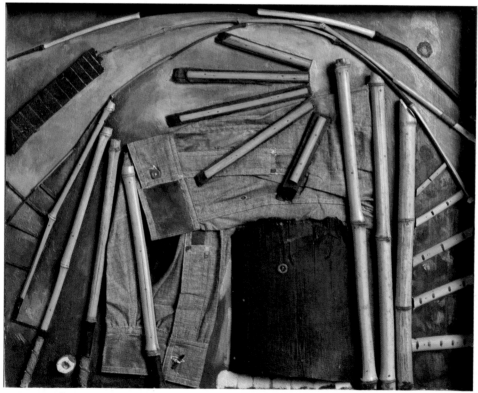

FIG. 6 Arthur G. Dove, *Goin' Fishin'*, 1926. Materials on composition board, 19 1/2″ × 24″.

During the next eight years, as he struggled to farm, Dove didn't paint very much. Stieglitz worried that Dove would stop painting entirely. However, several momentous occurrences took place. Dove's father died, freeing him from the difficult task of trying to please a strong parent while remaining true to himself. Also, he fell in love with Helen Torr, known as Reds, a painter who shared his passion about art. Leaving all his possessions behind, Dove ran off with Reds to live on a houseboat on the Harlem River. For many years they were unable to marry because Dove's wife refused to grant him a divorce or permission to see his son. But from that time onward he never faltered in his will to be an artist.

By 1924 Dove was experimenting with a form of art called assemblage, created by gluing bits of material such as scraps of cloth, metal, or paper, to the surface of a wood board. Since he was on a limited budget, Dove found assemblage both cheap and amusing to do. The texture, or sense of touch, in non-art materials attracted him. In *Goin' Fishin'* [FIG. 6] the composition includes denim shirtsleeves, a block of wood, and pieces of a bamboo fishing pole. The use of these humble found objects illustrates Dove's Yankee thrift, as well as his lighthearted, homespun sense of humor.

In 1929 Dove's wife, Florence, died unexpectedly. Dove and his son were reunited, and William confided that he wanted to be an artist like his father. The following spring Arthur and Reds went down to New York City Hall for a brief marriage ceremony with a dime-store ring. Afterward they opened a joint bank account and had lunch at the counter in Pennsylvania Station. More of a celebration would have been in order, but the country was sliding deeper into the Great Depression. The stock market had crashed, banks had failed, and the economy was in ruins. Thousands lost their jobs and their life savings. The unemployed gathered on every corner. A whole generation in America would grow up knowing deprivation.

The couple struggled, yet they managed to keep their sense of

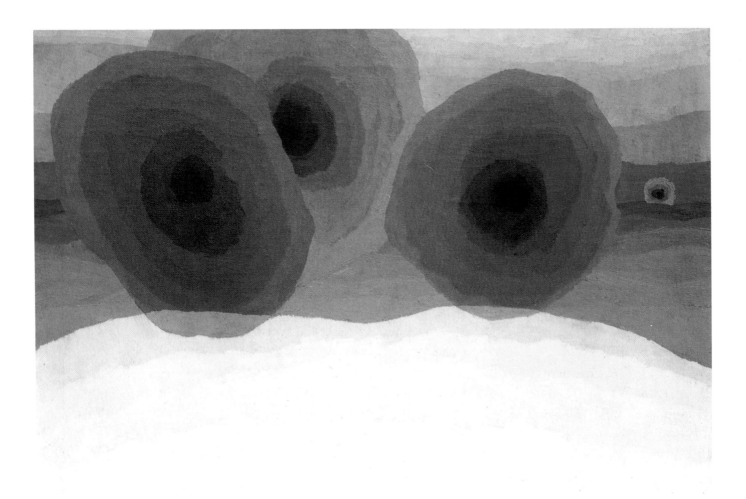

FIG. 7 Arthur G. Dove, *Fog Horns*, 1929. Oil on canvas, 18" × 26".

humor. "Mother speaks of sending Reds some jewels to keep as family treasures instead of any money for Christmas," Dove wrote Stieglitz. "A bag of wheat would be far more interesting than jewels on Christmas." He and Reds moved into a yacht club on Long Island, where they lived rent-free, working as caretakers. Views of the ocean and sky stimulated some of his best work.

In his seascape *Fog Horns* [FIG. 7], simple, round shapes pulsate and throb to create the sensation of sound—the eerie quality of foghorns echoing from the sea. The association of two senses in art, in this case the suggestion of sound through a visual image, is called synesthesia.

By overlapping the circles, Dove creates a sense of depth; the muffled blasts move toward the viewer through the haze. The soft colors of mauve, gray, and blue combined with the swelling forms produce a feeling of calm—the mysterious solitude of night and sea.

To get much-needed financial support, Dove might have joined the Works Progress Administration, called the WPA. This program, established by the government during the depression, provided jobs, and supported many of Dove's fellow artists. But Dove was unwilling to be dependent and refused to become a part of the WPA. Stieglitz came to his rescue by arranging to send him a fifty-dollar-a-month stipend from the steel magnate and art patron Duncan Phillips, in exchange for artwork. In retrospect, Phillips, who amassed the largest collection of Dove's work, benefited most from the arrangement.

After spending five years back in Geneva, where Dove managed his family's property, he and Reds settled into a cottage on Long Island Sound. As he was closer to New York, he could go in to visit Stieglitz and see the paintings of friends, especially Georgia O'Keeffe, an artist he admired. Although his health began to fail, he continued to work at his craft.

At a time when the public favored realism, Dove's intimate studies of nature seemed too modern. A market always existed for narrative paintings, but Dove went on creating his quiet abstractions. He had equated realism in art with America's obsessive love of material wealth. It took courage to paint the way he did, despite poverty and lack of commercial success.

Eventually his work was shown in many major exhibitions, including ones at the Philadelphia Museum of Art and the Museum of Modern Art in New York. In 1946 Alfred Stieglitz died, and Dove's death from heart failure followed four months later. This marked the end of an era in American art, but Arthur Dove left a legacy that celebrated the American landscape and foreshadowed the rise of abstract painting in the 1950s.

3

GEORGIA O'KEEFFE

1887–1986

"A WOMAN ON PAPER"

Georgia O'Keeffe, like Arthur Dove, drew her inspiration from her feeling for the land, in her case the flat Midwestern landscape where she grew up. Her paintings were sometimes abstract, at other times realistic. Like Dove, she almost never painted human figures, but unlike his earthy palette, her forms vibrate with sumptuous color. She disliked being called a "woman artist," believing that her art should not be categorized, but her character, as well as her work, still speaks to women today.

All her life, Georgia O'Keeffe did things her own way. If her sisters wore ribbons, she wore her braids plain; if they wore white stockings, she wore black. She didn't want to look like anyone else; she didn't want to be like anyone else. She was herself, Georgia.

She was born in 1887 on a farm in Sun Prairie, Wisconsin. Fertile, gently rolling fields stretched as far as the eye could see in every direction. The huge prairie sky dwarfed people, animals, and buildings, reducing them to specks on the landscape. Georgia's first memory was of "the brightness of light—light all around." This impression of light and space from her childhood, together with the matter-of-fact connection to things of the earth natural to life on a farm, influenced her work all her life.

Georgia, the second child and oldest daughter, often said she was the only person she knew who had had a happy childhood. The

O'Keeffe children went to a one-room school on the farm, and the closest town was a long buggy ride away. Still, Georgia learned to play the piano and the violin and took drawing lessons.

Her world seemed happy, solid, and secure, but big changes were coming. Her father tired of the bitter Wisconsin winters, and her mother wanted better educational opportunities for the children. They sold the farm and moved to Williamsburg, Virginia.

Georgia went to boarding school and, after graduation, studied at the Art Institute of Chicago and then for a year at the Art Students League in New York City. She learned to paint in the traditional, conservative style of the Art Students League's most renowned teacher, William Merritt Chase. At the end of the year she won a prize for the best still life and a scholarship for a summer of study.

Then she went home to hard reality. The move to Williamsburg had been the beginning of a downward slide for the O'Keeffe family. Her parents couldn't afford another year of school, so in 1908 Georgia went to Chicago to begin earning a living as a commercial artist, doing illustrations for advertisements.

Four years later, back from Chicago, O'Keeffe lived with her mother and sisters in a boardinghouse they ran for students in Charlottesville, Virginia. She no longer painted. There didn't seem to be anything she wanted to say with her art—or any way to say it. She said, "If one could only reproduce nature, and always with less beauty than the original, why paint at all?" Luckily one of her sisters persuaded her to take an art class at the University of Virginia with a teacher named Alon Bement.

Georgia O'Keeffe photographed in front of one of her paintings by Alfred Stieglitz.

Listening to Bement, O'Keeffe heard something that sparked her imagination. Bement taught the Arthur Wesley Dow system of art. This method stressed flowing lines, organic forms, and a balance of light and dark masses. O'Keeffe seized on these fresh ideas and began to work again.

Bement helped her in practical matters, too. His recommendation helped her get a job teaching art in Amarillo, Texas, despite her lack of a college diploma. In time, he encouraged her to go back to New York to study further at Columbia University's Teachers College.

At Columbia the twenty-seven-year-old O'Keeffe stood out from the other students; she was poorer, more serious, and more certain of what she wanted. She wore plain black clothes and lived in a small, stark room, but her paint and brushes were the best available.

O'Keeffe had visited Alfred Stieglitz's gallery 291 while she attended the Art Students League, but she had found Stieglitz intimidating. Now she went again with a fellow art student, Anita Pollitzer. While the warm, outgoing Anita made friends with Stieglitz, Georgia quietly looked, listened, and absorbed what this enthusiastic man said about art.

That fall of 1915 O'Keeffe took a teaching position in South Carolina. She wrote to

Anita Pollitzer that she had pinned up all her work on the walls of her room and given herself a private art show. "I have things in my head that are not like what anyone has taught me—shapes and ideas so near to me—so natural to my way of being and thinking that it hasn't occurred to me to put them down."

Several times in the next few months Georgia sent rolls of new drawings to get Anita's reaction, with stern instructions not to show them to mutual friends, teachers, or anyone. On New Year's Day Pollitzer wrote a confession to the artist. Against O'Keeffe's instructions she had taken the most recent drawings to Stieglitz .

Her letter continued: "I went with your feelings & emotions tied up & showed them to a giant of a man who reacted—'finally a woman on paper. . . . I'd know she was a woman—look at that line. . . . Tell her they're the purest, finest sincerest things that have entered "291" in a long while.' " It's not too surprising that within two months O'Keeffe went to New York to take a class at Columbia.

FIG. 8 Georgia O'Keeffe, *Special No. 9,* 1915. Charcoal on paper, 25" × 19 1/8".

She didn't go to see Stieglitz—from shyness or pride—until someone came up to her in the school cafeteria and asked whether she was the "Virginia" O'Keeffe whose drawings were on exhibit at 291. O'Keeffe hurried downtown to confront Stieglitz about hanging the work without asking—or telling—her.

He persuaded her to let the drawings stay up. Although the almost exclusively male art world didn't take women artists seriously, Stieglitz was an exception. He had been looking for an American woman artist to join the select group at 291. In Georgia O'Keeffe he found the artist he sought. The abstract yet organic shapes of draw-

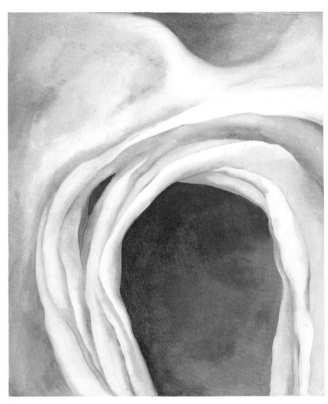

FIG. 9 Georgia O'Keeffe,
Music Pink and Blue I, 1919.
Oil on canvas, 35" × 29".

ings such as *Special No. 9* [FIG. 8] fit Stieglitz's theories about the artist's expression of personal spirit through abstract forms.

O'Keeffe still had to earn a living, and she went to Texas to teach. The flat Texas landscape, which most people found bleak and harsh, inspired her. She wrote enthusiastic letters to Stieglitz about the big Texas skies and the wind that scoured the earth. The correspondence continued, and within a year, Alfred Stieglitz and Georgia O'Keeffe moved in together. He was fifty-four. She was thirty-one.

Inspired by her unique beauty, he began a project of his own, a *Portrait* of the woman who now shared his life. For it, he took hundreds of photographs of both O'Keeffe and her work. She was his model, a familiar role for women in art, but he committed himself to the artist as well as the woman.

Gallery 291 had closed in 1917, but Stieglitz found other gallery space, and in January 1923 he presented "One Hundred Pictures, Oils, Watercolors, Pastels, Drawings by Georgia O'Keeffe, American," the first public show of her work since 1917. She joined the choice list of other Stieglitz "native-born" discoveries, including Arthur Dove, whose work O'Keeffe found most sympathetic to her own. In his publicity Stieglitz made much of O'Keeffe's "Americanness"—referring to her farm girlhood and her time in Texas—and minimized her artistic education. He claimed that her painting was instinctive, "a woman on paper."

The many new paintings included abstractions such as *Music Pink and Blue I* [FIG. 9]. She said she had done the music series when she remembered a class at Columbia in which the students listened to music and painted their impressions. The powerful shapes of pink, cream, and white, modeled with light and shadow, lead to a limitless blue void. The swelling arches seem to pulse with music, but critics looked at this and other abstract paintings and interpreted them as a woman's paintings about her most intimate sexual feelings.

The research of Sigmund Freud, the great German pioneer in psychoanalysis, had recently been published in English. Freud had written a scholarly work, but some of his theories about the unconscious mind were quickly transformed into popular culture. Half the public was thrilled: the other half was outraged to hear that their unconscious minds seethed with thoughts of freedom and pleasure that their conscious minds "repressed" with manners, customs, and social politeness. Getting in touch with the unconscious became the stated goal of many in the arts—and trying to read the unconscious meaning of an artist's work became the goal of the critics and public.

The sexual interpretation of her paintings gave O'Keeffe mixed feelings about all the attention they attracted. On the one hand, she wryly said that most people bought paintings with their ears, not their eyes. She knew that all the sensational talk helped her sales, but the stories and reviews made her feel vulnerable and exposed. She didn't think the real Georgia O'Keeffe had much in common with the one the newspapers wrote about.

After the reviews of those early years, however, she decided to choose more subjects from the real world rather than "shapes that exist in my head" like *Music* and *Special No. 9*. She had painted realistic flowers before. Now she began the new series of flower paintings that became some of her most appealing work [FIG. 10]. Because of the tightly cropped, close-up point of view, the clean, curving shapes of the white lilies can be seen as an abstract composition. O'Keeffe insisted that she painted flowers the way she saw them. The critics could write what they liked about the feminine symbolism.

FIG. 10 Georgia O'Keeffe, *Calla Lily,* 1930. Oil on board, 6″ × 4 2/3″.

Because they lived together, O'Keeffe's life changed to fit Stieglitz's established habits. They spent winters in New York City. In the summer they went to Lake George, New York, where the whole Stieglitz family shared a house. Unfortunately, after a few years the Lake George scenery Stieglitz loved to photograph no longer provided enough stimulation for O'Keeffe's paintings. She complained that the mountains and enfolding landscape looked too lush and green, too pretty. When Stieglitz absolutely refused to change his routine, the self-reliant O'Keeffe took a train west.

New Mexico dazzled O'Keeffe. She bought her first car—a Model A Ford—and learned to drive so that she could explore this sparsely settled country. Here was the space, the huge sky she craved. Nearly every spring after that she went west, alone. She bought both a ranch—called the Ghost Ranch—and a house in the small town of Abiquiu, New Mexico. Each winter she returned to New York and Stieglitz with cases of new paintings.

Sometime in the first years of her travels Georgia began incorporating the bleached bones she found on the desert into her paintings. In *Cow's Skull: Red, White, and Blue* [FIG. 11], the compelling shape of the cow skull fills the canvas against a background of vertical stripes. The folds of blue shaded into white suggest cloth or perhaps another radiant sky. The outstretched horns of the skull and the long shape of the head could be a crucifix.

O'Keeffe didn't discuss the meanings of her paintings except in the most matter-of-fact terms. If the skulls reflected personal worries about death, or a political response to the Great Depression then raging across the United States, it remained a private matter.

O'Keeffe's artwork went out of fashion during the 1950s, but one of the advantages of a long life is the opportunity to outlive your critics. In the 1960s she was rediscovered by a new generation of American painters who responded to her brilliant colors and simple shapes.

Her strong-minded dedication to her art also made her a perfect

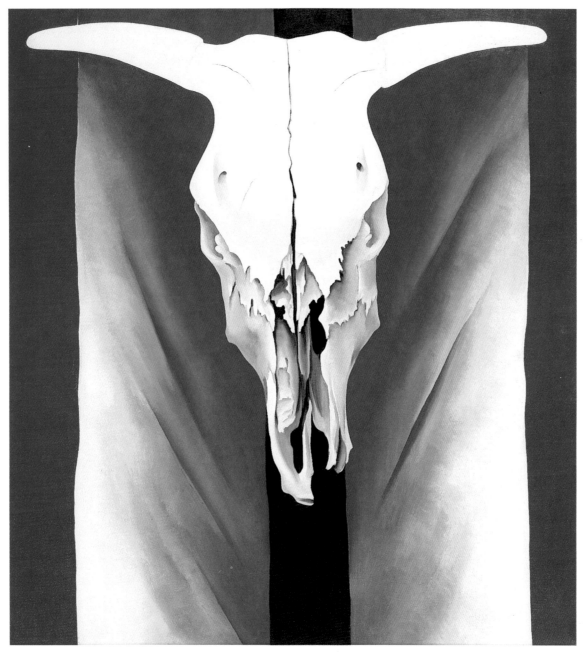

FIG. 11 Georgia O'Keeffe, *Cow's Skull: Red, White, and Blue*, 1931. Oil on canvas, 39 7/8" × 35 7/8".

role model for the growing feminist movement. O'Keeffe had been a feminist all her life, but she usually refused to be a spokesperson. She wanted to paint, not give speeches. The people who turned up at her door were a nuisance, and she often lost her temper with them. "What can you say to visitors, especially to aspiring artists?" she asked. "Go home and work!" or else, "Nobody's good at the beginning."

She continued to work in New Mexico until she was in her nineties, when her sight failed. She died at age ninety-eight. By then the girl from Sun Prairie had become an American icon, seen as part of the pioneer tradition: an original talent, proud, independent, still fiercely herself—Georgia O'Keeffe.

4

EDWARD HOPPER

1882–1967

THE PAINTER OF AMERICAN REALISM

Edward Hopper's color tended toward low-key tans, ochres, and greens. His figures could look awkward. Georgia O'Keeffe committed herself to filling space in a beautiful way; Hopper seems hardly to have thought of beauty. The impact of his paintings comes from a different kind of beauty, one drawn from psychological truth. No one before or after him has so powerfully captured the experience of loneliness and isolation Americans felt as the country went from a rural to an industrialized society.

Edward Hopper was a tall man, more than six feet four, lanky, square-jawed, and solemn. Even after he became one of America's most famous artists, with his picture on the cover of *Time* magazine, he didn't talk much. He said, "If you could say it in words there'd be no reason to paint. The whole answer is there on the canvas."

Today the Hudson River village of Nyack is a suburb of New York City. In 1882, the year of Hopper's birth, it was very different. Horses and wagons traveled the dirt roads. The trade of the village depended on the railroad, and on the hundreds of boats, large and small, that went up and down the Hudson.

From the windows of his family's house, young Edward could see the busy riverfront. Three blocks away, he visited bustling shipyards, where he watched skilled workmen building racing yachts. At one time he thought of becoming a marine architect—a designer of boats. This ambition may have had less to do with his own desires than with his parents' hope that all his drawing and painting would lead to a practical career.

His father owned a dry goods store in Nyack. Hopper worked there sometimes, but he was not pressured to follow in his father's footsteps. From his early childhood, his mother encouraged him in his artistic pursuits—a marionette theater, drawing, and painting. Not that Hopper needed much encouragement. At age six he used the blackboard he'd received for Christmas as an easel. A little later he signed his name in his first paintbox, followed by the inscription "would-be artist."

He built model boats and, as a teenager, a small catboat to sail on the river. Modest all his life, he ignored the fact that this represented a big project for a fifteen-year-old and said it didn't sail very well. His father had given him the materials so that Hopper would spend more time outdoors, but building a boat didn't change anything. He preferred his own company and spent most of his time sitting in the attic, drawing and painting. People who remembered him from that time recalled a shy, tall, gawky boy whom they called Grass Hopper because of his long awkward legs.

Edward Hopper with his older sister Marion.

After graduating from high school he spent a year at the Correspondence School of Illustrating in New York City, then transferred to the New York School of Art. There he met Robert Henri, whom he later described as "the most influential teacher I had." Henri urged his students to search out everyday subjects in the city life around them, not the romantic or conventionally scenic ones. Hopper learned this lesson well, but it would be many years before he translated it into successful paintings.

In 1906 Hopper, like Arthur Dove, went to Europe to finish his painting education. Seven years later, the work of European painters who were then in Paris would explode on the New York art scene at the Armory Show, but Hopper continued to work in a realistic style. If he saw abstract and cubist works, they didn't affect him. However, as he was always sensitive to light, he said the light in Paris wasn't like any he had ever seen—even the shadows were luminous.

Back in New York, Hopper became one of many painters making a living by illustrating for newspapers and magazines. He didn't like the work and often walked around the block several times before going into a client's office; he needed the money, yet did not want to draw what or how other people wanted him to draw. Still, he supported himself that way for about twenty years, illustrating three days a week and doing his own paintings and etchings the other four. He preferred working for business and trade magazines because they wanted illustrations of topics he would explore in a more serious way in his paintings. For example, his illustration [FIG. 12] for the magazine *Hotel Management* and the painting *Chop Suey* [FIG. 13] both show people dining. The illustration suggests glamour and exuberance; the painting depicts intense yet mundane "real life."

FIG. 12 Edward Hopper, jacket illustration for *Hotel Management*, January 1925.

Beyond the figures of the two women waiting for their meal at a Chinese restaurant you can see through the window to a portion of the Chop Suey sign and the street. Hopper called this "seeing the outside and the inside at once," and it appears in varying ways in many of his works. The seemingly casual composition, reminiscent of a snapshot, also is characteristic. The profile of the woman dining at the table in the background sticks

FIG. 13 Edward Hopper, *Chop Suey*, 1929. Oil on canvas, 32″ × 38″.

into the left edge of the painting, looking as randomly cropped as a tourist's photograph, but it was carefully planned by the artist. The woman's hat and red mouth form the apex of the composition's strong triangular lines.

A small painting of a sailboat, accepted for the 1913 Armory Show, sold for $250, but Hopper didn't sell another painting for ten years. He had several other shows in that time, including his first one-man show at the Whitney Studio Club (the beginnings of what is now the Whitney Museum

FIG. 14 Edward Hopper,
House by the Railroad, 1925.
Oil on canvas, 24″ × 29″.

of American Art), but there were no sales. A less determined man might have grown discouraged.

In 1923 Hopper's luck changed. He spent the summer in Gloucester, Massachusetts, a New England seaport full of the Victorian buildings he loved to paint. Josephine Nivison, the student who had posed for their teacher Robert Henri's painting *The Art Student* [see FIG. 1], happened to be among the many painters there. She persuaded Hopper to try watercolors.

When the Brooklyn Museum invited Nivison to exhibit her watercolors in the fall of that year, she talked them into looking at the work of her good friend. In the exhibition his watercolors hung next to hers. The critics loved him and ignored her.

Encouraged, Hopper went back to Gloucester the next year—after marrying Jo Nivison. That fall he had his second one-man show, the first in a commercial gallery. All the paintings sold—as well as five others not in the show. At age forty-two he had achieved an overnight success. He promptly quit illustrating to devote himself full-time to his art.

The subjects he explored throughout his life are familiar to most Americans. He painted the architecture of houses and buildings in the city and in the country, modest restaurants he and Jo frequented, theaters and movie houses they enjoyed attending, and waterfronts of New England towns similar to the Nyack of his childhood. At first glance, they are ordinary scenes.

The early painting *House by the Railroad* [FIG. 14] could be one of a thousand places where America's past and future meet. The large Victorian house looms above a railroad line, a sign of progress and new technology that runs horizontally across the canvas. The harsh sunlight reveals the empty windows with half-drawn shades and throws strong shadows, heightening the feeling of isolation. The dramatic light communicates a sense of tension, as if something momentous is about to take place.

If we look a little longer, we see that the house has not completely surrendered to time. There is a sense of underlying strength here. The roof is whole and the pillars still stand. The glowing red chimneys hint that life, tough and enduring, remains beyond the shadowed door.

Unlike most Americans during the Great Depression, Hopper was starting to make money. By 1933 he had been honored with a retrospective exhibit of his paintings at the Museum of Modern Art. But he and Jo lived thriftily, seeing money only as a means to their goal of artistic freedom. After their marriage they shared the same apartment on Washington Square North where Hopper had been living for ten years—although they rented a studio for Jo. They shopped for inexpensive clothes and wore them until they fell apart. They bought their first car, a secondhand Dodge, drove it till it wouldn't run any more, then bought another secondhand car. In the summer they moved from their unassuming apartment in New York to a small house in South Truro, Cape Cod, where they stayed until early November.

Sometimes Edward and Jo Hopper took car trips, looking for new subjects to paint. Hopper was interested in the experience of traveling and life on the road rather than conventional panoramic beauty. His typical landscape contained a building—a house, a bridge, a gas station, or a lighthouse—and often some evidence of a road or railroad. The landscape of *Western Motel* [FIG. 15] is seen from a typical, anonymous motel window, past the hood of a car. In the foreground, looking directly out of the canvas at the viewer as if posed for a camera, sits a woman. Jo, who was an actress as well as an artist, modeled for all her husband's paintings of women, both young and old.

Hopper worked slowly, making many sketches and studies before beginning an oil painting. By his own choice he led a quiet life. For him all the excitement he needed lay in the challenge he faced in front of the canvas.

FIG. 15 Edward Hopper, *Western Motel,* 1957. Oil on canvas, 24″ × 29″.

When asked whether he had a favorite painting, Hopper named *Second Story Sunlight* [FIG. 16]. The subject matter, point of view, light, and psychological tension are all elements common to many of Hopper's works. The subject is an ordinary scene in a small New England town. The point of view is that of a passerby catching a glimpse of other people's lives. The strong, direct light emphasizes the spare, repeated shapes of the buildings and gives a sense of heightened emotions. The girl leans forward as if expecting—or yearning for—a visitor. Whom does she look for? What is the older woman's role? Is she guarding the young girl or simply watching?

Hopper didn't provide any answers. He resisted the idea that his paintings told stories. He said, "I was more interested in the sunlight on the buildings and on the figures than in any symbolism. . . . Any psychological idea will have to be supplied by the viewer."

When pressed he cautiously admitted that perhaps the critics who read loneliness and urban alienation into his work had guessed correctly, that he was a loner. But he refused to go further. The answers, Hopper insisted, were in the paintings.

In them he gave unsentimental, clear-eyed dignity to the unremarkable lives of the Americans he chose as subjects. Hopper said, "A nation's art is greatest when it most reflects the character of its people."

FIG. 16 Edward Hopper, *Second Story Sunlight*, 1960. Oil on canvas, 40" × 50".

5

THOMAS HART BENTON

1889–1975

CHAMPION OF THE AMERICAN SCENE

Determined to create a native art that would surpass European traditions, Thomas Hart Benton championed regionalism, a movement glorifying American subject matter. Abstract works by such artists as Arthur Dove and Georgia O'Keeffe didn't appeal to him. He wanted to paint, both in style and subject, paintings that would be understood by ordinary people. As the Great Depression took over the nation, he tried to capture what America had lost—tradition, homespun values, and respect for the past. Benton's murals, his most impressive work, tell the story of a country coming of age. His twisting figures and landscapes are supercharged with American energy.

A popular hero in his day, Thomas Hart Benton cultivated a frontier manner complete with boots, crude language, and barroom brawling. His hotheaded statements and art world high jinks often made headlines. Benton once said, "I want to be as important to Americans as the funny papers."

As a boy, Thomas Hart Benton traveled around Missouri with his father, known as the Colonel, who was campaigning for Congress. Often the Colonel would introduce him to the crowd as a future lawyer or politician, but already, at the age of seven, Tom displayed a strong talent for drawing.

Even though his father bragged about his son on the road, at home he found fault with everything Tom did, especially his need to spend hours by himself sketching. The Colonel gave Tom long history books to read and lectured him on laziness and scribbling. Benton once wrote, "Dad was profoundly prejudiced against artists and with some reason. The only ones he had ever come across were the bootlicking portrait painters of Washington. He couldn't think of a son of his having anything to do with their profession."

However, Tom hardly fit the stereotype of the artist his father imagined. Although he was small, he loved fighting and had an

FIG. 17 Thomas Hart Benton, *Katy Flier, Vinita, Oklahoma,* **1898. Pencil on paper.**

opinion about everything. Where his drawing was concerned, he refused to give up. "I used to go out in the woods, or the barn, and sit for hours, nursing my dreams in silence. . . . My first pictures were of railroad trains. Engines were the most impressive things that came into my childhood. . . . I scrawled crude representations of them over everything" [FIG. 17].

His mother, Lizzie, a musical Southern beauty, promoted her son's artistic talents. She and the Colonel disagreed on other subjects as well. The clashing dreams of Benton's two strong-willed parents set the stage for his lifelong tendency toward drama and conflict. During most of his childhood, the Benton family rotated between rural Neosho, Missouri, and Washington, D.C., where his father served in Congress for eight years.

In the capital Lizzie worked at becoming a successful society matron. Colonel Benton disapproved of his wife's "fancy ways," and many arguments erupted in the household. The Colonel was also fighting another losing battle. Dedicated to keeping the United States an agricultural country, but unable to stop the trend toward industrial development, he eventually lost his seat in Congress. The family returned to Missouri for good.

The summer Benton turned seventeen, he found a job as an artist, drawing cartoons for a newspaper in the lead mining town of Joplin, Missouri. At the end of two happy months, Benton begged to study art. Instead, his father packed him off to a military school. Except for when he was playing football, Benton didn't fit in with the other students at the academy. He festooned his letters home with cartoon sketches to demonstrate his artistic skills. Finally, with the help of an understanding English teacher, he persuaded his father to let him go to the Art Institute of Chicago a year later.

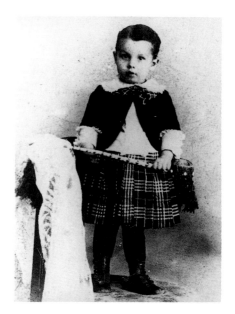

Thomas Hart Benton, age three.

Chicago in 1907 was a progressive city filled with automobiles and skyscrapers. Benton rode the streetcar to school and ate in small diners or beer gardens at night. He found art classes frustrating and had a hard time taking criticism. "I'm beginning to think there's no such thing as a born artist," he wrote to his mother. Later he said, "From the moment I first stuck my brush in a fat gob of color I gave up the idea of newspaper cartooning. I made up my mind I was going to be a painter."

Like many other young Americans, Benton took off for Paris after art school. Although he lived the bohemian life of an artist, with a studio apartment and all-night conversations at outdoor cafés, his paintings, which imitated the impressionist style popular in Paris, received little attention. Eventually his mother came to Paris and threatened to stop sending his allowance if he didn't go back to Neosho.

Benton headed instead to New York City, where he painted his way through a number of styles, including abstraction, as in *Constructivist Still Life* [FIG. 18]. He later renounced these early efforts as experimental. To make a living, he designed movie sets and painted portraits of movie stars. Then he found a job teaching art for fifty dollars a month at the Henry Street Settlement, and he also gave lessons in the neighborhood. There he met his future wife, Rita Piacenza, an Italian immigrant, who was seventeen and a student in his classes. Struck by her beauty, he made a plaster bust of her as a gift. (Years later, after they were married, she took the bust with them wherever they lived.)

To avoid being drafted and sent overseas during World War I, Benton joined the U.S. Navy in 1918 to work as an architectural draftsman. As he drew the activities he observed around him, his focus changed from what he termed "aesthetic drivelings and my morbid self concerns" to more objective interests. "I left for good the art-for-art's-sake world in which I hitherto lived. Although my technical habits clung for a while, I abandoned the attitudes which generated them and opened thereby a way to a world which, though always around me, I had not seen. That was the world of America."

FIG. 18 Thomas Hart Benton, *Constructivist Still Life*, 1917–18. Oil on cardboard, 12 1/2″ × 8″.

After his stint in the U.S. Navy, he returned to New York to resume his painting career and his romance with Rita. They were married in 1922. In *Self-Portrait, South Beach* [FIG. 19], we see a handsome but serious young couple whose noble stance and classic beauty have a modeled, sculptural quality. Benton had been studying the old masters and imitating some of their techniques, including making clay models of his subjects before painting them. Bathing attire might seem unusual for a self-portrait. But this painting, a salute to youthful power and idealism, reveals the artist's image of himself as a modern-day Greek warrior. Benton and Rita spent many summers in Martha's Vineyard,

FIG. 19 Thomas Hart Benton, *Self-Portrait, South Beach*, 1922. Oil on canvas, 49 1/2" × 40".

off Cape Cod, where this portrait was painted, and the island's beaches, boats, and bathers provided images for many of his finest works.

Throughout the next years, he achieved the recognition he craved. He had discovered the direction his work would follow—the American scene. When he returned to Missouri to see his dying father, he wrote, "I cannot honestly say what happened to me while I watched my father die, but I know that when, after his death, I went back East I was moved by a great desire to know more of the America which I had glimpsed in the suggestive words of his old cronies. . . . I was moved by a desire to pick up again the threads of my childhood."

The Ballad of the Jealous Lover of Lone Green Valley [FIG. 20], one of his later, more mature works, represents Benton's definition of American scene painting. Immediately recognizable as an American subject in an American location, this painting shows a typical rural landscape that could be anywhere in the Midwest. No one would confuse it with a European setting. The imagery in these paintings, Benton said, "would carry unmistakably American meanings for Americans and for as many of them as possible."

So strong are the sensory details of this painting, we could be right there watching the drama. In the lower section three country musicians play a popular tune (the title of the work) while above them the words of the song are played out. A woman clutches her chest as the menacing figure of her lover leans toward her with a bloody knife. The moon rises between them. Swirling bands of color draw our eyes up and around the canvas. Shape is an important element in Benton's work. He gives a feeling of movement and creates mood by repeating irregular forms. The distorted shapes add to the melodrama. Even the gnarled tree seems to writhe in fear.

Benton didn't limit himself to country scenes. He also painted mythological and biblical themes, and many historical and autobiographical murals, which are large scenes painted directly on a wall or on panels attached to a wall. Like Edward Hopper's paintings,

FIG. 20 Thomas Hart Benton, *The Ballad of the Jealous Lover of Lone Green Valley,* 1934. Egg tempera and oil on canvas, 42 1/2" × 53 1/4".

Benton's murals offer familiar, often ordinary images of America. However, while Hopper's paintings show scenes frozen in time, moving us into a world of private emotions, Benton's murals work in a different way. Our eyes jump from one element to another. There is no single central image, as in more traditional paintings. In one of his most important public commissions, *Social History of Missouri* [FIG. 21], we view a sequence of historical events, composed of rhythmic forms. Using this all-over approach to composition, Benton captured the restless energy of America.

These murals on the walls of the Missouri State Capitol caused great controversy. Legislators said the twisted bodies, distorted

FIG. 21 Thomas Hart Benton, *Social History of Missouri,* 1935-36 (detail of mural).

shapes, and barrage of visual stories disturbed their peace of mind. Critics called Benton a "literary stinkpot" and "a public nuisance." Benton, who loved to cause a ruckus, gave numerous press conferences at which he traded feisty insults with his opponents. A few years later the installation of a large Benton painting of a realistic nude at the Saint Louis Art Museum drew such crowds that the director had to rope the painting off.

Benton's ability to stir up trouble extended to fights with artists, including Stuart Davis; with newspapers; and with the public, especially in New York. When he moved back to Missouri to become director of painting at the Kansas City Art Institute, the *New York Sun* announced, MR. BENTON WILL LEAVE US FLAT—IS SICK OF NEW YORK AND

Thomas Hart Benton painting a self-portrait.

EXPLAINS WHY. Benton said, in his typical outspoken style, "I'm leaving New York to see what can be done about art in a fairly clean field less riddled with verbal stupidities. . . . I've been here twenty-one years and that's too long for any American to stay in one place. Do you think I am going to escape stupidity in the Midwest? Of course not. Wherever people talk, idiocy survives."

Although his students in Kansas City adored him, he made some damaging statements about certain colleagues at the Art Institute, which caused him to be fired. At times his opinions were outrageously prejudiced, but he remained unapologetic about them all his life. In his writings and speeches he railed against art that did not stress a recognizable image. He thought abstract art would be a short-lived fad. Benton's painting was in the tradition of American realism, which had always appealed to the practical, down-to-earth side of the American personality. Although Benton did not revolutionize American painting, his student Jackson Pollock did achieve this goal in the late 1940s and early 1950s.

Until he died in 1975, Thomas Hart Benton lived in Kansas City with his wife, Rita; their son, Thomas; and their daughter, Jessie. He continued to paint murals and easel paintings that told stories of American life. From his rolling Ozark landscapes to his bustling scenes of industrial progress, from portraits of country yokels to city slickers, Benton's message came straight from the heartland of America.

6

STUART DAVIS

1894–1964

PAINTER OF THE JAZZ AGE

New York City provided the stimulus for Stuart Davis's paintings; he liked jazz, bright lights, and action. In Edward Hopper's paintings, we glimpse a moment in time. In Thomas Hart Benton's, we picture a story or anecdote. In Stuart Davis's, many moments and stories converge. His canvases are filled with symbols of American culture on the move—neon signs, a newspaper, a pack of cigarettes, slang [FIG. 22]. For Davis, a true American art lay not in glorifying the American scene, but in changing its form.

S tuart Davis's father illustrated the bedtime stories he told his son, stories he made up as he went along. He expected Davis to do the same for his little brother, Wyatt. Unlike both Arthur Dove and Thomas Hart Benton, Davis was encouraged to become an artist. When he decided to quit school to study art at the age of sixteen, his parents, both artists themselves, readily gave their permission. A child prodigy, he achieved success at an early age. "In writing autobiographical sketches," he wrote, "it is not unusual for artists to dwell on the obstacles they had to overcome. . . . I am deprived of this profound satisfaction." Only later, because he turned to abstraction in his painting, did Davis struggle to be recognized.

Philadelphia, where Davis was born, was a thriving center for the arts. His father worked as the art editor and as a cartoonist for *The Philadelphia Press*. In those days disaster and crime stories were illustrated, and artists

FIG. 22 Stuart Davis, *Lucky Strike*, 1924. Oil on paperboard, 18″ × 24″.

such as William Glackens, John Sloan, George Luks, and Robert Henri worked for Stuart Davis's father. By the early 1900s these artists had moved to New York, where they exhibited together in a show titled "The Eight." They painted life as they saw it in a casual, intimate way.

Robert Henri had opened his revolutionary art school, and it was there that young Davis went to study. He learned from Henri that "art was not a matter of rules and techniques. . . . It was the expression of ideas and emotions about the life of the times." With fellow students, Davis explored the streets, the music halls, and the saloons, "riding, walking, and gadding about all over the place. . . . The pianists were unpaid, playing for the love of art alone . . . but the big point with us was that in all of these places you could hear the Tin Pan Alley tune turned into real music for the cost

FIG. 23 Stuart Davis, *Landscape, Gloucester,* 1922. Oil on canvas, 12″ × 16 1/8″.

of a five cent beer." Later Davis distilled the syncopated rhythms of jazz into his paintings.

During his first year of art school, the budding artist exhibited one of his pieces in a show with The Eight and, later, five watercolors in the Armory Show of 1913. After he saw this groundbreaking exhibition, he was exhilarated by the possibilities it presented. He said, "That settled it. I would be a modern artist. So easy. Except for one small matter: I was nineteen then. Fourteen years later, I would still be working on that little matter."

After art school Davis tried a regular job, joining the staff of a radical magazine, *The Masses,* but he resigned in protest when the editor insisted on dictating the content of his illustrations. He also managed to have several one-man shows and spent his summers painting in Cape Cod. At

FIG. 24 Pablo Picasso, *Glass and Bottle of Bass,* 1914. Charcoal, pencil, india ink, white gouache, newspaper, and woodblock-printed papers pasted on wood pulp board, 20 5/16″ × 26 11/16″.

first he traipsed around the countryside with his paints and easel but soon abandoned this practice in favor of quick sketches with a fountain pen. Back in the studio he used these drawings as starting points for paintings.

In 1918, during World War I, Davis served as a mapmaker for U.S. Army intelligence. Charting land and dividing it into areas might have stimulated his later interest in arranging the space in his paintings into blocks of color. For instance, in his painting *Landscape, Gloucester* [FIG. 23], he was moving toward abstraction via broken shapes and areas of color. Yet there are also recognizable images, such as the boat, cloud, and rocky beach.

Davis admired the work of the European modernists, especially Picasso, who were painting in a new style called cubism [FIG. 24]. Like the cubists, Davis fragmented the forms of the objects he painted, but his subject matter was pure Americana—gas pumps, stop signs, and jive talk.

His images became even more abstract a few years later in a group of paintings he titled The Egg Beater Series [FIG. 25]. "I nailed a rubber glove, an electric fan, and an eggbeater to a table, and stuck to that single subject for a whole year," he said. After painting this still life over and over again, he began seeing the objects only as relationships of color, shape, and line.

In 1928, when two of his paintings sold for the undreamed-of price of $900, Davis went to Paris. There he rented a small apartment, paying only $80 for a full year. When he wasn't roaming the streets of Paris, he spent most of his time in the studio painting his memory-based "mental collages," as he called them. He also surprised his family by courting a young

Stuart Davis as a teenager in New York.

woman from Brooklyn named Bessie Chosak. His parents didn't approve of the match, but, true to his independent nature, Davis married her anyway.

Bessie and Stuart returned to New York to face a national disaster—the Great Depression. Ironically, modern artists, who for years had barely been able to scrape by because of the public's rejection of their work, now fared somewhat better by working on various WPA programs. Despite economic problems, New York—with a population of nearly seven million people and with skyscrapers, elevated trains, and automobiles everywhere—was the most cosmopolitan city in the United States. Over the next four years, Davis filled his canvases with urban images—trains, signboards, cigarette packs, and cars. In Davis's paintings these objects exist as signs and symbols of America's new Jazz Age, fragments he combined into dynamic compositions.

During the 1930s one of his murals, which pictured the history of communications, was exhibited at the World's Fair in New York. Yet thousands of people who flocked by this mural did not know who Davis was. "The public is no better than an omelet," he said angrily. "Some people just don't celebrate. Not because they're poor; I'm poor. Not because they're ignorant; I'm ignorant. But just because they don't want to learn."

In 1934 Davis began to work for the WPA. Shortly after that his wife, Bessie, died tragically. This was a sad time for Davis, and for a while he used darker colors and denser shapes in his paintings. But by 1937 he energetically started work on a large mural, *Swing Landscape* [FIG. 26]. It was painted for a low-income housing project as part of the WPA program, though it was never installed. If we look closely at *Swing Landscape*, we can make out nautical elements—masts, buoys, spirals of rope, and small buildings on the shore. Davis created a jumble of carefully interwoven color combinations. Sequences of circles, stripes, and dashes overpower the underlying harbor scene. Everything is related. Lines thicken into forms. Looping lines travel about the canvas. Bold shapes bounce

FIG. 26 Stuart Davis, *Swing Landscape,* 1938. Oil on canvas, 86 3/4" × 172 1/8".

off one another. Davis balanced this topsy-turvy scene by repeating these elements of color, shape, and line. A riot of action and color, *Swing Landscape* captures the pulse of a busy seaport.

In 1938, the same year he completed *Swing Landscape,* Davis married Roselle Springer, an artist from New York, with whom he had his only child, James Earl. Davis also immersed himself in politics; he became chairman of the Artists' Congress, a group dedicated to protecting the rights of artists. Modern art, he believed, could stimulate a change in politics and promote social reform. He advocated art that would appeal to the masses, but attacked the American scene painting of Thomas Hart Benton, calling it a cliché. The two artists engaged in a lifelong rivalry, punctuated by verbal battles in the press. Davis was constantly being called upon to defend modernism. Yet he remained a lone figure who had more in common with jazz musicians than with fellow artists.

After the depression, Davis's work for the WPA ended, and, he wrote, "having no money I did the conventional things—hired a studio and devoted myself to painting." He also taught at the New School for Social Research in New York, where many rising young artists, including Romare Bearden, took his classes. This was a traumatic time in Davis's life; despite the number of gallery shows in which he participated, few collectors bought his work. The humorous punning in his titles, such as *Rap at Rappaport* and *Something on the 8 Ball*, might have masked the deep anger he suffered at being undervalued for such a long time.

In 1943, to celebrate the opening of a new group of paintings at a New York gallery, Davis threw a bash at a famous restaurant, Romany Marie, complete with heaping platters of spaghetti, bottles of red wine, and stimulating conversation. At the opening a week later, critics, artists, and collectors mingled to the live sounds of Duke Ellington and other jazz greats, who dropped by to serenade their friend "Stu." This set the stage for Davis's notoriety. His new works were a smash success, not only with buyers, but with critics and art historians. Friends remembered him that night—a short man with a cigarette dangling out of the corner of his mouth, who observed his newfound success with a wry smile.

The time was right. America was awakening to jazz and to modern art as well. World War II revived the country's patriotic spirit. Davis's art, animated by the signs and symbols of America, began to appeal to the public. He won awards, and museums around the country exhibited his works. One of his paintings was reproduced on 600,000 Pepsi-Cola calendars for 1945, and *Look* magazine named him one of the ten best artists in America. How did this affect Stuart Davis? The young man who had once frequented all the nightspots in New York, the fiery social activist who had given speeches and organized artists' strikes in the 1930s, retreated into his studio, living in modest seclusion. Despite all the acclaim, Davis's most compelling drive was his art.

In the 1950s Davis reexamined and updated the earlier concerns of his work, continuing to draw from memory on the canvas, as well as to incorporate some of the motifs that appear in his earlier notebooks. His paintings moved toward a greater simplicity, as seen in *Night Life* [FIG. 27], with bold colors and spare geometric shapes. At the same time, abstract expressionism was revolutionizing American art. Despite his retrospective at the Walker Art Center in Minneapolis and a second Guggenheim Museum International Award, emerging artists, intent upon breaking new boundaries, saw Davis's art as out of step with the times. Plagued by ill health, Davis quietly painted his way into the 1960s. He died of a stroke in 1964. Only today is his historical importance clear: In 1992 *The Washington Post* proclaimed, "He brought jazz to modern painting, led the way to pop art, and caught this country's glare and beat as no one had before."

FIG. 27 Stuart Davis, *Night Life*, 1962. Oil on canvas, 24" × 32".

7

ROMARE BEARDEN

1912–1988

COLLAGE OF MEMORIES

Because Romare Bearden celebrated African American culture through his paint-
ings, critics often called him "America's most important black artist." For years
he struggled to be accepted as an artist without such qualifiers. At the same time,
he fought hard to get recognition for black artists. Although his work vividly
expresses the rich traditions of his heritage, he also portrayed the effects of racism
and poverty. For this reason he is sometimes considered one of the social realists,
artists of the 1930s and 1940s whose paintings and photographs brought injus-
tice to the public's attention. But Bearden's most important work spans the 1950s,
1960s, and 1970s and chronicles the black experience in America as he lived it.

It all began on a quiet street in Charlotte, North Carolina, where Romare, the only child of Bessye and Howard Bearden, was born in the second-floor bedroom of his great-grandparents' house. Next door stood his great-grandfather's grocery store, and farther down, the train trestle and railroad bridge leading to the main station. The cotton mill took up a whole block. Huge wagons piled high with sacks of raw cotton lined the streets. Born into slavery, Romare Bearden's great-grandfather was a self-made man who belonged to the black upper class of Charlotte. Both Bearden's parents were college-educated.

As a child in Charlotte, Bearden loved to watch the train go by the Southern Railroad station on West Trade Street. The big gunmetal-blue steel locomotive, with its coal cars, Pullman drawing room and sleeping cars, and caboose, seemed magical as it carried people to faraway places. Bearden later said, "You could tell not only what train it was but also who the conductor was by the sound of the whistle." Years later train imagery would appear in many of his collages, such as *The Afternoon Northbound* [FIG. 28].

The Bearden family. Young Romare is in the middle of the first row.

Light-skinned, with blond hair and blue eyes, Bearden turned heads as a child. One day his parents took him shopping in a white neighborhood and passersby made racist remarks to his father. After this incident, and because jobs for African Americans had dwindled in that area of the South, Bearden's parents decided to go North in hopes of finding a better life.

His father took a job as a steward on the Canadian railroad. On and off during the next ten years Bearden lived in Harlem with his parents and in Pittsburgh, where his mother's parents lived. He spent summers in Charlotte with his father's family. Bearden's life in Harlem offered a sharp contrast to his country summers in Charlotte. Harlem in the 1920s was becoming a predominantly black neighborhood, but the public school he attended was a melting pot for Italian and Irish immigrants as well. There were gang fights and racial tensions. Bearden was often mistaken for white, which caused him trouble with both sides.

But the city was an exciting place to live, with the sounds of jazz all around. From pianos and record players to the street musicians on every corner, music filled the air. In their apartment, Bearden's father often played the piano with such famous jazz musicians as Fats Waller and Duke Ellington. His father had found a new job with the Public Works department; his mother, Bessye, edited a weekly African American newspaper. For the most part the Beardens led a comfortable life.

FIG. 28 Romare Bearden, *The Afternoon Northbound,* 1978. Mecklenberg County series, collage on board, 15 1/4″ × 20 5/8″.

The summer Bearden was twelve he went to live for a year with his grandmother, Carrie Banks, in Pittsburgh. She ran a boardinghouse near the steel mills for blacks from the South who came up looking for jobs. The furnaces were so hot that his grandmother had to rub the men down with cocoa butter when they came home scorched from the fire. One afternoon while Bearden was shooting marbles with his friends, a boy with braces on his legs came into the yard and stood watching. The other boys began teasing him but were scolded by Mrs. Banks. Afterward Bearden and the boy, Eugene, became friends. Eugene was such a good artist that Bearden's grandmother set up a table so that Eugene could teach him to draw. A year later Eugene died, but during their brief friendship, Eugene had inspired Bearden to draw and observe details, a lesson he never forgot.

When he was in high school, Bearden returned to Pittsburgh to stay with his grandparents. He showed more interest in baseball than in art. But his parents insisted that he go to college. The tuition money for his first year came from an unlikely source.

Romare Bearden in his studio.

It was the period known as Prohibition in the United States, when buying or selling alcoholic beverages was against the law. Speakeasies, clubs that sold illegal liquor (known as bootleg), were all the rage. A bootlegger named Druett gave Bearden a job in his speakeasy collecting money from the waiters who sold liquor to customers. One night thieves held up the club and robbed the cash register. Most of the money, however, was stuffed in Bearden's pants pockets. Druett was so appreciative, he handed the teenager enough cash to send him to college for a year.

At Boston University, Bearden played baseball on an all-black team. Although there were no African Americans in major-league baseball at that time, he was told he could pass for white if he wanted to join a professional team. He declined. After two years he transferred to New York University. His mother tried to discourage his increasing desire to be an artist; she wanted him to be a doctor, but by the time he graduated, he was bent on following his chosen path.

In the 1930s he moved into his own apartment and met other young black artists, writers, and musicians who were gravitating to Harlem. To support himself Bearden took a job as a caseworker with the Department of Welfare in New York. He also had his first show of paintings and met Stuart Davis, who taught him how to bring the spontaneity of jazz to his painting. Bearden described the rhythm in his work as similar to the pulse in jazz, "the use of space, of silence." Swing bands and musicians inspired many of his most joyous paintings, as in the later work *Wrapping It Up at the Lafayette* [FIG. 29]. Here Bearden divided the canvas into four sections, packing each part with the swirling movement, vibrant color, and swinging sound of black music.

Just when he finally could afford his own studio, Bearden went through a period during which he could not paint. His cleaning lady, a short, homely woman named Ida, noticed that the same piece of brown paper had been sitting on his easel for weeks. She suggested that he use her as a model. "I know what I look like," she said, "but when you look and can find what's beautiful in me, then you're going to be able to do something with that brown paper of yours." She began posing for him, which inspired him to start painting again. This experience sparked his lifelong preoccupation with painting the black female form.

In 1942, during World War II, Bearden enlisted in the army, serving in an all-black regiment. In those days the army was segregated. After his discharge at the rank of sergeant, he found an apartment in the same building that housed the famous Apollo Theater, where some of the great jazz and swing bands of New York were among the talented performers.

Despite a few shows of his paintings, Bearden went through a difficult time. His mother had died in 1943, and he was unable to make a living as an artist. He returned to his job at the Department of Welfare, which he kept for three decades. It allowed him to support himself and to paint at the same time. It also gave him a

FIG. 29 Romare Bearden, *Wrapping It Up at the Lafayette,* 1974. Of the Blues series, collage with acrylic and lacquer on board, 44 1/8" × 36".

FIG. 30 Romare Bearden, *The Street*, 1975. Collage on board, 37 1/2" × 51".

closer view of the poor, whose stories and faces appear, portrayed with great sympathy, in his later work.

In the 1950s, Bearden went to Paris to visit friends, many of whom were artists, writers, and musicians who had moved there after World War II. The city filled his head with new ideas, sights, and sounds. He took French lessons, roamed the museums, and visited other artists' studios. He loved the freedom and lack of racial prejudice in France and applied for a grant so that he could stay and paint. But when it did not come through, he returned to New York.

He had no luck selling his new paintings, so he turned to songwriting. One of his songs, "Seabreeze," rose to the top of the record charts. Yet he suffered bouts of depression, stomachaches, and an inability to paint. He soon was hospitalized because of a nervous breakdown.

One evening at a charity benefit in Harlem, he met a beautiful young dancer, Nanette Rohan, who changed his life. They fell in love and were married in 1954. Nanette encouraged him to start painting again. The couple moved out of Harlem into a larger space downtown, on Canal Street. At his new studio Bearden concentrated on building his skills. One of the ways he learned technique was to imitate the style of the old masters; he wrote about this process in his book *The Painter's Mind*. In addition, he and Nanette began to spend time in the Caribbean. He attributed the vivid color and images of native folklore in paintings such as *Wrapping It Up at the Lafayette* to their trips there.

During the 1960s the civil rights movement was in full swing. African Americans were demanding a long-overdue end to discrimination, reforms in voting rights, and desegregation of schools. Although Bearden's work had begun to be recognized, he saw that the white arts establishment ignored black artists. He formed the Spiral Group with twelve other artists to help their cause.

An experiment with the Spiral Group led to a new creative period for Bearden. At one of their meetings he spread cut-out photos from magazines on the floor. The idea was to make a group picture by pasting the bits of paper on a large sheet of posterboard. Although the other artists lost interest, Bearden decided to use the technique in his own work.

His first collages, which he described as the art of "putting something over something else," portrayed scenes of contemporary African American life. There is a strong documentary quality in his painting titled *The Street* [FIG. 30]. Depicting a scene in front of a tenement building, the picture is built up with photographic images, faces, and bodies lifted out of their original context. Figures of varied sizes and expressions crowd into the space. Each tells a different story. Their lives are literally pasted together, bound by Bearden's memory of the neighborhood of his youth.

Perhaps his most famous painting of Harlem is *The Block* [FIG. 31], a large six-paneled collage. Three panels show a funeral and a group of storefront shops at street level, complete with a parked car and onlookers; on the second story the bricks have been removed so that the interior scenes are visible. The brownstones are arranged as if they are separate blocks of color, and may remind us of a piano keyboard. To create the aura of Harlem for viewers, a tape of street sounds and church music accompanied *The Block* when it was exhibited at the Museum of Modern Art in New York.

Bearden's collages became his breakthrough works, catapulting him to fame. He won awards, including the National Medal of Arts from President Reagan in 1987, and many museums mounted retrospectives of his work, including the Mint Museum of Art in Charlotte, his childhood home. In his later years he illustrated children's books; designed sets for dance companies and plays; and drew a backdrop for a Hollywood

movie. Throughout his long career, Bearden never turned back from his vision, at the center of which was a strong social conscience.

In 1988, at the age of seventy-six, Bearden died of bone cancer. In his will he made provisions for a foundation to encourage and support talented African American art students. His body of work is not only an inspiration to young artists, but also a testament to the diversity of cultures in the United States. Through his visual autobiography, melding influences from jazz to African art, Romare Bearden helped to bring the black experience into the mainstream of American art.

FIG. 31 Romare Bearden, *The Block,* 1971. Collage of cut and pasted paper and paint on masonite: six panels, 48″ × 216″ overall.

8

ISAMU NOGUCHI

1904–1988

WEST MEETS EAST

Isamu Noguchi went from realistic portrait busts to abstraction in sculpture, moved by the same ideas that influenced Arthur Dove, Georgia O'Keeffe, and Stuart Davis to explore abstraction in painting. Like Dove and O'Keeffe, Noguchi was drawn to nature and the spiritual side of art. He was one of the first American artists to use the materials he worked with—stone, wood, bronze, and paper—as the subject matter of the work itself.

In 1917, thirteen-year-old Isamu Noguchi, his suitcase full of carpenter's tools, traveled by himself from Japan to the Interlaken School in Indiana. His American mother, a writer and teacher named Leonie Gilmour, had heard that the school's theories of applied education—boys learning through doing—matched her own. She decided it was time for her son to become acquainted with America.

Though born in the United States, Noguchi was only two years old when his mother moved to Japan to be closer to his father, Yone Noguchi, an internationally known Japanese poet. Yone Noguchi provided a house for them and wrote an article about his son's arrival, but eventually he married a Japanese woman and started a new family. His involvement with Isamu's life and early education in Japanese schools was small.

Isamu Noguchi did not have an easy time in Japan. His light eyes gave away his half-Caucasian parentage, and the conservative Japanese were no more welcoming to mixed-race children than people in the United

States would have been. He was teased and shunned by his schoolmates.

Leonie Gilmour had tried several different schools for Isamu before sending him back to the United States. When he was ten she even tutored him herself for a while because she had decided they would build a house together. She wanted to prepare Isamu with practical skills to face what she must have known would be a difficult life. At the same time she apprenticed him to a cabinetmaker to learn the use of traditional Japanese tools. These were the carefully wrapped tools he brought with him on his long trip from Japan to Indiana.

The ocean voyage was exciting. So was the train ride from the West Coast across the vast mountains and prairies to Indiana. He had grown up with the Japanese view of nature, an intense awareness of the details of a leaf, a flower, or an insect. Now he saw the huge American landscape with its sweep and panorama. The contrast between these two views of the world, the two sides of Noguchi's heritage, and his wish to reconcile them, would provide artistic inspiration for the man, but the boy had other, more pressing problems.

He arrived at the small train station in Rolling Prairie to find the school about to close. The grounds and buildings had been turned over to U.S. Army troops training to fight in World War I. Isamu had no money and nowhere else to go, so the soldiers adopted him as a kind of mascot. When the troops departed for Europe, Isamu was left behind. He camped out in the abandoned buildings with two caretakers until he was rescued by Dr. Rumely, the former head of the school. Rumely became his mentor and placed the boy with a family in the nearby town of LaPorte. There, under the Americanized name Sam Gilmour, he attended the local high school for three years.

From early childhood Noguchi's ambition was to be an artist, so after graduating from high school he apprenticed with a well-known sculptor. Within three months, thoroughly discouraged by the sculptor's evaluation of his work, Noguchi left to go to Columbia University. If he had no talent for art, he would study medicine.

The pull of art remained strong. With the encouragement of his mother, who recently had returned to the United States, he began taking evening classes at the Leonardo da Vinci Institute in Greenwich Village. There he learned the old-fashioned technique of stonecutting. A star pupil, he soon exhibited his work. He began frequenting Stieglitz's gallery to see the current American modernists, including Arthur Dove and Georgia O'Keeffe, and to join the continuing conversation about the aims and direction of contemporary art.

Isamu Noguchi (in his Paris studio) at work on a portrait bust.

Eventually Noguchi left Columbia to concentrate full-time on his sculpture. He received a fellowship and spent a year in Paris, where he made friends with other American artists living there, including Stuart Davis. During that time he apprenticed himself to the distinguished modernist sculptor Constantin Brancusi, whose bold abstractions changed Noguchi's vision of what sculpture could be.

Back in New York in 1929 and faced with earning a living, Noguchi became a portrait artist whose busts became fashionable and much in demand. His financial success and the help of a fellowship gave him the chance to travel again.

He planned to visit Japan, but before he left, his father wrote and told him not to come using the last name Noguchi. What Yone Noguchi didn't say was that in the political climate of Japan, having a half-Caucasian son was an embarrassment. Isamu was in Paris when he got the letter. He was hurt, but he decided to go anyway, though he rearranged his plans to include many months in China.

In his autobiography Noguchi wrote, "I don't know whether fortune or misfortune is the better teacher." This trip provided both. In some ways it was tense and difficult. An outsider in America and Europe because he had a Japanese father, he now felt equally an outsider in Japan. He saw his father, but it was never to be a warm or close relationship. To leave the difficult family dynamics behind, Isamu traveled around Japan, slowly becoming acquainted with the art community there. The present was too painful, so he took refuge in Japan's past.

In the ancient Japanese capital of Kyoto, he studied ceramics with an illustrious potter. For several months he stayed in the cottage of a ditchdigger while he worked in the pottery studio and explored the quiet, dusty corners of the city. Kyoto was not yet a tourist mecca, and he found the famous gardens in disrepair, but fascinating and unlike any Western garden he had seen. He began to think about the gardens as a kind of sculpture. Like sculpture, they had three dimensions and needed to be seen from many different vantage points to be fully appreciated. The novel idea occurred to him to sculpt a whole landscape instead of creating sculpture as objects within a landscape.

Noguchi returned to New York determined to integrate some of these new concepts into his art. But his one-man show of sculpture was not a critical success. Luckily an old friend, the dancer Martha Graham, came to the rescue with the suggestion that he design sets for one of her new productions. Aware of the distinctive way Graham's dancers moved, he

FIG. 32 Isamu Noguchi, *Humpty Dumpty*, 1946. Ribbon slate, 58 3/4" high.

approached the stage as if it were a piece of sculpture. He translated some of the mythic and ritualistic aspects of Noh theater, the classic Japanese dance-drama, which he had seen in Japan, into the first of more than twenty symbolic sets he designed over the next decade.

In December 1941 Japanese planes bombed Pearl Harbor. People of Japanese extraction who lived in the western United States were rounded up at gunpoint and sent to a series of "relocation camps" for the duration of World War II. It did not matter that many of these people were American citizens, had lived in the United States for years, spoke only English, and had houses, businesses, and families. They were seen as security risks.

Noguchi was not rounded up. He volunteered to go to a camp in Poston, Arizona, with plans to make it a more livable place. He didn't need to be there long to see that his objectives were hopeless. With some difficulty, he left and tried to find other patriotic work. Frustrated in his wish to help, he retreated to a new studio in Greenwich Village.

He began work on a series of sculptures carved from leftover pieces of thin marble and slate used for facing buildings. The rounded shapes, abstract yet implying life, are associated with European and American surrealist artists of the 1930s who used these biomorphic forms to suggest dreamlike, unconscious states. The pieces of the sculptures fit together after the fashion of traditional wooden Japanese houses and temples, which are snugly assembled with notches rather than nails, glue, or welding. *Humpty Dumpty* [FIG. 32] and similar works solidified Noguchi's growing reputation.

FIG. 33 Isamu Noguchi, *Ikiru (To Live),* **1952. Concrete bridge railing, Hiroshima, Japan.**

THE AMERICAN EYE

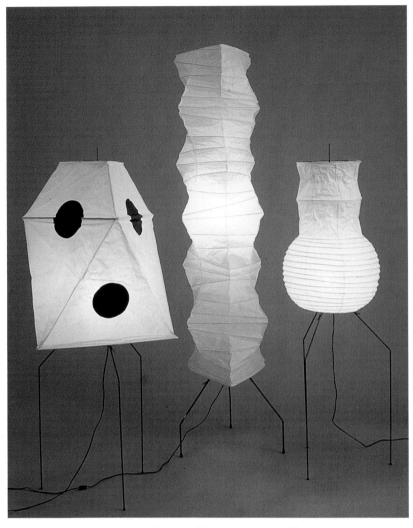

FIG. 34 Isamu Noguchi, *Akari*. Mulberry paper and bamboo.

In 1950, Noguchi went back to Japan. This visit differed from the earlier one. Now he was an established artist with an international reputation, not a promising beginner. And in post-World War II Japan, as in America, there was more interest in modern art. Noguchi's father, Yone, died in 1947, and Noguchi created a sculpture for his garden memorial. Noguchi was asked to design several public spaces, including two bridges at Hiroshima [FIG. 33]. The bridges were part of the Peace Park built in memory of those who died when the United States dropped an atomic bomb there in the closing days of the war. Noguchi's bridges put into practice his belief that sculpture could function practically as well as aesthetically.

He proved his point again when he updated designs for traditional paper lanterns. Noguchi called his lamps *Akari* [FIG. 34] after the Japanese word for "light." Made of bamboo covered with mulberry paper and formed into startling new shapes, they influenced design throughout the world.

About this time, Noguchi met a beautiful Japanese movie star named Shirley Yamaguchi. They were married in 1952. Five years later they divorced. It was his only marriage.

Noguchi put his artistic beliefs to a different test in 1956 when he won a commission for the large plaza around the UNESCO headquarters in Paris [FIG. 35]. Here he was given the opportunity to explore his dream of a sculptural garden that links areas with water and plantings as well as sculpture. To Westerners the garden looked Japanese, with its carefully placed stones (stones that in fact Noguchi imported from Japan, where he found large boulders worn by river water into fantastic shapes). To the Japanese the garden looked Western. The master gardener Noguchi brought from Japan to help with the plantings said, "The things in Japanese gardens that should be motionless Isamu reverses."

Making UNESCO's garden with its carefully considered monolithic stones, flowing water, and plants helped Noguchi to clarify his ideas. He said, "UNESCO was my beginning lesson in the use of stone." The search for stones, and other developments in his work, strengthened his artistic ties to Japan, and he established a studio there in addition to his studio in New York. Looking for the right stones for his gardens and plazas was always an exciting part of a project for Noguchi, one of the things he said "got me going."

He had begun his career carving portrait heads. Now, at the end of his career, Noguchi was interested in letting the materials themselves be his

FIG. 35 Isamu Noguchi, *Jardin Japonais*, 1956–58. UNESCO Headquarters, Paris.

FIG. 36 Isamu Noguchi, *The Stone Within*, 1982. Basalt, 75″ high.

subject rather than transforming them into something else. In *The Stone Within* [FIG. 36] he peeled away part of the oxidized covering of a basalt boulder to show the shiny interior. Here there are a variety of textures—the stone as it is found in the natural state, as it appeared when he chipped away the rusty skin, and finally the polished stone. As he reveals three aspects of the stone, he reminds us of the process of making the artwork—from the monolith to the finished piece. The history of his thinking and of the stone are part of *The Stone Within*.

Noguchi went his own way in art, with few direct followers. However, much that seemed radical about his sculpture—earth art, sculpture as part of an environment, and the history of an artwork becoming part of the reason for the piece—is now part of the artistic vocabulary that contemporary artists use. The serenity and quiet power of his art grew out of the struggle to blend Eastern and Western traditions and introduced a fresh point of view into the American art world.

Isamu Noguchi at work in his studio.

9

DAVID SMITH

1906–1965

SCULPTOR OF THE GRAND STATEMENT

David Smith invented forms never before seen in American sculpture. Like Isamu Noguchi, he found beauty in the raw materials he used to make his art, fashioning his sculpture from cast-off metal and rusted farm tools. He attained mythic status among a new generation of American artists who continue to create large-scale sculpture out of welded steel.

For someone who didn't remember seeing art as a child other than "a very, very dark picture with some sheep at the public library," David Smith's ambition to be an artist by the time he was in high school is surprising. It could be because his ancestors were pioneers and he inherited their independent, robust spirit.

Smith's grandfather was a blacksmith who had founded the town of Decatur, Indiana, where David was born in 1906. His father, an inventor, managed a telephone company. New technology, railroads, and the automobile were changing small towns all across America. "When I was a kid, everyone in town was an inventor. There must have been fifteen different makes of automobile in Decatur. . . . Two blocks from where I lived there were guys building automobiles in an old barn. Invention was a fertile thing then."

However, his family had little interest in artistic invention. Once his mother tied four-year-old David to a tree to keep him from wandering out of the yard; there he modeled a lion out of mud. His mother praised his cleverness, but other than that he never received any encouragement from her to make art. A straitlaced Christian who preached piety and hard work, she hoped he would become a teacher. Talk of drinking, dancing, or gambling was strictly taboo. He saw his father as hardworking and unaffectionate.

Smith resented staying home to do household chores on Saturday mornings while the rest of his friends were outside playing, but he did learn the value of a dollar and hard work. He often found refuge from his family's strict rules at his grandmother's house. She gave him an illustrated Bible, which he kept always. The Egyptian photographs in the back became the source of later artworks.

He loved to draw cartoons in high school and sent away for a correspondence course in drawing. His classmates nicknamed him "Bud" after the cartoonist who created *Mutt and Jeff*. Smith was known not only for his witty cartoons but also for his pranks; he once set off a cannon in the middle of town. At Ohio University, he took art courses but complained that they were useless. "I was required to use a little brush, a little pencil, to work on a little area, which put me in the position of knitting—not exactly my forte." He transferred to Notre Dame but left two weeks later—he had somehow failed to notice the lack of art classes in the catalog.

That summer he worked as a riveter on the assembly line at the Studebaker automobile factory in South Bend, Indiana. "Did it strictly for the money—more than I ever made in my life," he said. But that experience provided him with skills he was to use later as a sculptor. When the company promoted him to the banking division, he was transferred to New York. Smith asked his landlady there for the name of a good art school, and she referred him to one of her other boarders, Dorothy Dehner. An artist herself, Dehner directed him to the Art Students League, where he studied for five years.

David Smith and Dorothy Dehner became friends and soon fell in love. An orphan raised by three aunts with modern notions of childbearing, Dehner had traveled in Europe and acted in the theater. To Smith, the beautiful young woman represented everything his ordinary background lacked. They married a year later at New York City Hall.

At first the couple lived compatibly, but even then Smith showed signs of a short temper. Once he accidentally spilled milk on the table, and when Dorothy yelled out in surprise, he ripped the tablecloth off and hurled the dishes at the wall. He then went out and threw himself into the freezing Hudson River. Over the years his violent spells became more frequent.

The artistic community thrived in New York in the early days of their marriage. The Museum of Modern Art was founded in 1929, and a number of European artists had moved to the city. At this time Smith also discovered Freud's theories on the importance of dreams as a guide to our true wishes and feelings. This became a strong force in his painting. Throughout his career he practiced free association in his work, moving back and forth between his conscious and unconscious mind. He discovered that art could be made of many different forms, "from found discards in nature, from sticks and stones and parts and pieces." He believed there were no rules to follow, only the conviction of the artist.

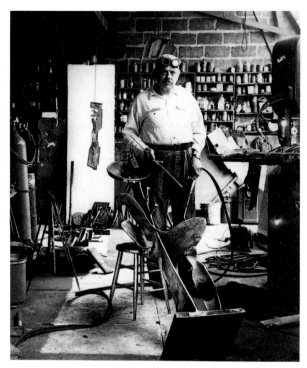

David Smith at work in his studio.

During an eight-month trip to the Virgin Islands in 1932, Smith roamed the beaches, collecting lumps of coral and beach debris. He made his first sculpture from a piece of coral. Other works from 1932 included a fragile assemblage of coral, wire, and wood, which he painted red, blue, and yellow [FIG. 37]. Back in New York, he bought his first welding torch and began combining different materials such as cast bronze or flat sheet metal with bars of steel.

Smith used the couple's small apartment in Brooklyn as a workshop. While he was welding, Dorothy followed him around with a sprinkling can to douse the fires. Finally one morning as they took a walk on the Navy pier, she spotted a long shack called the Terminal Iron Works and suggested he do his work there. The next day, the big Irishman who ran the place told him to move right in. The area near the ironworks teemed with activity—ships loading, barges refueling, and ferries tied up to the dock. Soon Smith knew everyone on the waterfront; the workmen taught him their skills, played chess with him, and never made fun of the iron and steel constructions he called sculpture.

During these depression years, Smith said, "Life was hard," but he and Dorothy managed to maintain a car, pay the rent, and keep their farm at Bolton Landing, a property they had bought in upstate New York.

In 1938 David Smith had his first one-man show, and in the next four years, while making his constructions, he worked on a series of bronze medallions titled the Medals for Dishonor. The public disliked the explicit anti-war imagery, which was Smith's own response to the advent of World War II. "Never sold a one," he wrote. "But I would rather have the approval of other artists and critics than monetary sales reward."

After working for the WPA, the Smiths decided to move permanently to Bolton Landing. Both artists wanted to live more self-sufficiently and to be able to work on their art uninterrupted by the hubbub of city life. Dorothy planted a vegetable garden, and David

FIG. 37 David Smith, *Construction*, 1932. Wood, wire, nails, and coral, painted red, blue, and yellow, 37 1/8″ × 16 1/4″ × 7 1/4″.

learned to hunt and butcher meat. However, the hundred-year-old house had no insulation or electricity and was bitterly cold in the winter. David used a shed down the road from the house as a studio; later he rebuilt it and named it after the Terminal Iron Works in Brooklyn.

By the end of 1941 the United States had entered World War II. The draft board rejected Smith; he had severe sinus problems. He felt relieved because he associated war with the violent side of his nature. This identity with violence, which he saw as brute masculine force, found its expression in his sculpture through the use of steel—a material he called both beautiful and brutal. He tried to curb his terrifying demons by working intensely in his studio. He sold a few sculptures, which allowed him to replace the mouse-infested old farmhouse. But Dorothy, discouraged by the isolation and cold winters, and by his erratic mood swings, moved back to New York. They eventually divorced.

As Smith's reputation grew, he received many offers of lectures and teaching positions, some of which he accepted, as he always needed money for his work. A grant allowed him to build some large stainless-steel pieces. He filled his stockpiles with discarded metal parts, which he began to use with more frequency in his sculpture instead of casting his own parts. One of his great innovations was to abandon the traditional pedestal on which a sculpture was placed and to integrate it into the piece.

Smith's second marriage to his student Jean Freas was celebrated in 1953 amid bags of grain in a feed store. Freas was attracted to the burly artist in his tweed suit and cap who preached the joys of artistic freedom. Their daughters, Rebecca and Candida, were born within a few years. Smith dedicated many sculptures to them, etching their names or initials into the metal. That marriage also broke up, and although his adored daughters visited him often in Bolton Landing, he was alone there much of the time. He began to make very large sculptures, placing them in groups in the meadow near the house.

In his journal he wrote, "I get so wound up at my work. I can't get

FIG. 38 David Smith, *Cubi IX*, 1961. Stainless steel, 105 3/4″ × 58 5/8″ × 43 7/8″.

sleepy and work through 3, 4, 5 or daylight. Did this back in Brooklyn. All my life the workday has been any part of the 24—on oil tankers, driving hack, going to school, all three shifts in factories. I'd hate to live a routine life."

In the 1960s Smith continued to explore some of the ideas that had preoccupied him over the years. He

David Smith looking over a snowy meadow filled with his sculptures.

started making series of related works, repeating images with variations in his sculpture. Titled the Zigs, Circles, Voltris, Wagons, and Cubis, these series were made concurrently over a short period. He combined contradictory forms and ideas in his work—flatness and volume, thinness and mass, or complexity and simplicity. Many of these works have a larger-than-life feeling and conjure up the rugged American landscape.

In *Cubi IX* [FIG. 38] the box-shaped elements of stainless steel are burnished to reflect the surrounding space. The light dances off the surface of the piece to create pattern and texture. There is a sense of precarious balance to these boxes, yet they are stacked almost playfully, suggesting movement. In traditional sculpture there is a unified, continuous flow from one view to the next. Smith did away with this sense of continuity and thus changed the definition of sculpture forever. If we were to walk around *Cubi IX*, each view of the piece would be completely different. This break with tradition was a goal of American artists, and the idea of discontinuity from one view to the next became a powerful tool for American sculptors in the 1960s.

The Voltri series, made in a factory in Italy for the first Spoleto Arts Festival in 1962, are workbenches and chariots fashioned from handmade tools and debris found lying around the factory. They indicate Smith's very American joy in tinkering. Other artists had incorporated found objects in their sculpture, but Smith used them in a revolutionary way. He celebrated an object's beauty without transforming it into something else [FIG. 39]. With these works, critics heralded Smith as one of the most significant artists of his generation. Museums such as the Museum of Modern Art and the Metropolitan Museum of Art began to collect his work, and he exhibited widely. At the height of his career, returning home late after a party, David Smith drove his truck off the road near Bennington, Vermont, and was killed. He was fifty-nine years old.

A hero to younger artists, Smith said, "Always remember that you are the artist, the creator. It is your own ego that is being satisfied. It is rewarding if others understand your aim, but it is never your duty to explain it. . . . Have the courage of your conviction—for you will never be happy being anything else."

FIG. 39 David Smith, *Voltron XX*, 1963. Steel, 62 1/4″ × 37 1/2″ × 26 1/2″.

10

JACKSON POLLOCK

1912–1956

ACTION JACKSON

Jackson Pollock took his teacher Thomas Hart Benton's theories about composition and activating the whole surface of the canvas and gave them a spin that turned the art world upside down. Pollock's large "drip" canvases were an original solution to the artistic problem of expressing thoughts and feelings without using a recognizable image. Other artists who were Pollock's contemporaries also tried to get what was inside their heads and hearts down on canvas in a totally abstract way. Critics named this group of New York painters abstract expressionists.

Visitors to the outdoor art show in Greenwich Village might have noticed a good-looking blond young man with a red bandanna tied around his neck, whose paintings were propped on the sidewalk. The prices were five and ten dollars. It was the first public showing of twenty-year-old Jackson Pollock's work. Fifty years later a single one of his paintings was to be auctioned for millions of dollars, but on that spring afternoon in 1932 there were no sales.

Jackson Pollock was born in Cody, Wyoming, in 1912, the youngest of five boys. Later, when he lived in New York, he proclaimed his Western heritage by walking around in cowboy boots, an unusual sight in those days on Manhattan streets. But in truth, within a year of his birth his parents, Roy and Stella Pollock, moved the family from Wyoming to San Diego, California. It was not their last move. At least eight times during his childhood the Pollocks picked up and started over, always believing that this time their luck would improve.

In 1928 the move was to Los Angeles, where Stella hoped the children would receive a better education than they could in the country. By then Charles, the firstborn and ten years older than Jackson, was in New York studying art. Charles had always been regarded by his family as the most talented of the five Pollock boys. Early in life he announced his plan to be an artist—an ambition encouraged by Stella. The younger boys looked up to and copied their big brother, who must have seemed impressively sure of himself in their shaky world.

Pollock attended Manual Arts High School in Los Angeles. Most of the other thirty-five hundred students were sports crazy—Pollock and his friends were not. They wrote a paper criticizing the values of the school and suggesting, "Instead of 'hit that line,' we should cry 'make that grade.' " Pollock probably didn't do much of the writing—he was more likely to punch someone who disagreed with him—but authorities saw him distributing the paper, and he took all the blame. After the rebels published a second critical paper, Pollock was expelled.

When he returned to school the following September, he had long hair and wore eccentric clothing to reflect his artistic aspirations.

Jackson Pollock at sixteen.

His fellow students had no tolerance for his appearance or his ideas—members of the football team held him down and cut off his hair. Soon after that he got into a confrontation with the coach; this time Pollock threw some punches. He was expelled again. Only through the intervention of his art teacher was he allowed to come back at all, and then just for two art classes. He would not get a diploma.

FIG. 40 Jackson Pollock, *Going West*, 1934–35. Oil on fiberboard, 15 1/8″ × 20 1/4″.

His brother Charles came to the rescue. Home for the summer after studying at the Art Students League in New York City with Thomas Hart Benton, Charles persuaded Jackson to return to the city with him, and in the fall of 1930 Jackson Pollock moved to New York, making the first of many cross-country car trips down the back roads of America.

Thomas Hart Benton and his wife, Rita, took the handsome young man under their wing and treated him almost like a son. By all accounts Pollock was not an obviously talented student. He had trouble controlling his paint and struggled at his drawing. What made his teachers single him out over technically better students was the expressiveness in his work; it had emotional energy and a compelling rhythmic quality.

In this student composition, *Going West* [FIG. 40], we can already see Pollock's variation on what Benton taught—a method of composing a painting that stressed rhythmic lines and shapes organized around imaginary vertical axis lines. The effect was of dynamic movement all over the canvas. Even after Pollock no longer painted realistically, these theories of composition guided his work.

The Great Depression made earning a living hard, but Pollock took only part-time jobs so that he would have time for painting. Then he was accepted into the artists' division of the WPA, the Works Progress Administration. The weekly salary allowed artists like Pollock, used to living frugally, to give up their jobs and concentrate on painting. A strong sense of community developed among these artists, a feeling that something exciting was happening in American art. At the same time New York City was enlivened by the arrival of artists who were fleeing turmoil in Europe.

These artists brought with them theories, helpful to Pollock, of the way the unconscious, dreams, and myths were used in paintings. He had already begun experimenting with some of these ideas after seeking therapeutic help for a problem with alcohol. Since Pollock was more comfortable with artistic than verbal expression, he made paintings for his doctors from his own dreams, fantasies, and childhood memories. He never stayed in therapy long enough to solve the problems that took him there, but he used what he learned to enrich his art.

In the early 1940s Pollock met two women who were to play critical roles in his success. The first was another artist—Lee Krasner. Both she and Pollock had been invited to be part of a prestigious show at a New York gallery, one that included established American artists such as Stuart Davis. If Krasner hadn't been a woman of determination, she wouldn't have come far in the macho New York art world. Wondering who this Jackson Pollock was and why she didn't know his work, she went to his studio. She was "bowled over" by his paintings. Whether it was the art or the artist that attracted her, within a few months they moved in together. Krasner put her own painting on a back burner while she concentrated on helping to build Pollock's career; it was a choice familiar to many women of her generation.

FIG. 41 Jackson Pollock, *Guardians of the Secret,* 1943. Oil on canvas, 48 3/8″ ×75 3/8″.

The second influential woman was an unusual collector and art dealer—Peggy Guggenheim. An American heiress, she had lived for most of her adult life in Europe, where she built an impressive collection of avant-garde paintings. World War II forced her to return home. Once in the United States, she opened a New York gallery called Art of This Century.

She offered Pollock a small monthly allowance as an advance against the sale of his paintings and scheduled his first one-man show, which was also her gallery's first show of a contemporary American painter. One of Pollock's paintings was sold to the Museum of Modern Art in New York. Another, *Guardians of the Secret* [FIG. 41], was later purchased by the San Francisco Museum of Modern Art.

In this painting Pollock still used recognizable—though not realistic—figures. A dog lies under a white rectangle that might be a tabletop or a tombstone, and a human figure stiffly guards each side of the canvas.

THE AMERICAN EYE

Pollock heavily overpainted these figures with other colors, shapes, and scrawled lines of pictographs and symbols. He told Krasner he wanted to "veil the image." The result could refer to a primitive myth, a dream, or a fragmented memory from childhood.

Lee Krasner decided Pollock needed a quiet place to work, away from the busy social life of New York. She persuaded him to look at a house on five acres of land far out on Long Island in an area known as Springs. The run-down house needed work—there was no bathroom indoors, no heat except from a woodstove in the kitchen, and no hot water—but with Peggy Guggenheim's help they bought it. With views of marshland and the Accabonac Bay, and room for two studios, it seemed like a perfect place for two artists to concentrate on painting. So in the autumn of 1945, Jackson Pollock and Lee Krasner married and settled down in the country.

Pollock thrived in Springs. Since boyhood he had had a strong, almost mystical feeling of oneness with nature, and the flat, marshy Long Island landscape with its beautiful, ever-changing light inspired him. He moved his studio from an upstairs bedroom of the house to a small, unheated barn on the property. It was there that he unrolled his canvas on the floor and began the paintings for which he is best known. He had been struggling for a long time to express what he felt directly, but

FIG. 42 Jackson Pollock, *Full Fathom Five,* 1947. Oil on canvas with nails, tacks, buttons, key, coins, cigarettes, matches, etc., 50 7/8" × 30 1/8".

abstractly, on the canvas. His solution to the problem was both simple and inventive.

He stopped using images entirely. Instead of applying oil paint with brushes, he poured and dripped ordinary house paint and industrial aluminum paint directly onto the canvas. *Full Fathom Five* [FIG. 42] is one of the first of these new paintings. In the surface, thickly covered with his carefully controlled lines, which cross and crisscross each other, he embedded tacks, nails, cigarette butts, pebbles, and whatever came to hand to add to the texture.

Pollock's paintings grew larger, and as he did in *Number 1, 1948*, Pollock sometimes let the unprimed canvas show in places [FIG. 43]. The evidence of the artist's movements became an important part of the final work. We can imagine his steps, the sweep of his arm and hand, and lariats of paint flung, dripped, and coaxed onto the canvas. The painting became a document of his movement and actions. The loops of paint look spontaneous, but Pollock had an underlying mental blueprint for his free-wheeling surfaces. He called his painting "energy made visible."

Large in scale—almost nine feet long—*Number 1, 1948* shows a series of deliberate handprints across the top, a primitive testament to the maker. Perhaps Pollock remembered taking a trip with his father to visit Native American ruins in New Mexico, where they found handprints hundreds of years old on the adobe walls of the pueblos.

In one of his few statements about his method of painting the unstretched canvas laid out on the floor, Pollock claimed Native American inspiration. He said he liked to be able to walk around a canvas and work on all four sides, "and literally be in the painting. This is akin to the method of the Indian sand painters of the West."

In August 1949, *Life* magazine published an article that gave birth to the Pollock myth. In the *Life* photograph Pollock looks like a rebel in his paint-stained jeans and boots, with a dangling cigarette and his "I don't care what you think" expression. The article played up Pollock's Western background and talked about his painting with a mixture of awe and

FIG. 43 Jackson Pollock, *Number 1, 1948,* **1948. Oil and enamel on unprimed canvas, 68″ × 104″.**

Jackson Pollock at work on a drip painting.

ridicule—but the publicity made his November 1949 show a triumph. Until then, interest in what was going on in postwar American art had been limited to a relatively small group of insiders. At the opening of Pollock's show, guests included the rich and famous from all walks of life, not just the usual friends and acquaintances from the art world.

While few artists copied his drip style, they did recognize his bold solutions to artistic problems that were preoccupying them all, and adapted them to their own work. The flatness of paint on canvas with no attempt to represent three-dimensionality, the alloverness, the lack of an image, the importance of the artist's gesture, and the huge size of the canvases would become the hallmarks of the modern American artists who had been newly christened abstract expressionists. In 1953 the Museum of Modern Art in New York sent an exhibition of American art on a European tour. The show, which included works by David Smith and Edward Hopper, as well as Jackson Pollock, let the world know that the distinctively American art dreamed of at the turn of the century had arrived.

Pollock had become well known, but fame was not the same thing as approval. Many people, including some of his fellow artists, privately and publicly criticized his work. Perhaps that is why he allowed photographer Hans Namuth to take pictures of him painting. The remarkable Namuth photographs, taken in Pollock's studio, show him working on *Autumn Rhythm*.

Namuth was so delighted with the photos that he persuaded Pollock to cooperate in the making of a short movie. Pollock was unhappy about the process. During the shooting he was overheard mumbling the word "phony." At a celebration the night the filming was finished, he started drinking heavily for the first time in several years. In a fit of rage he overturned the dinner table loaded with food and drinks onto his guests.

A few weeks later his annual show opened. The huge paintings crowded the walls and people jammed the gallery rooms—but they came to look at the controversial artist, not to buy. Today all these paintings are owned by museums, but then only one was sold—at a reduced price.

Pollock would do other great paintings in the next few years, but he had lost his momentum. The public romanticized his antisocial antics, while the critics said his best achievements were behind him. Four years after the *Life* magazine piece appeared, the brief glory days were over. Pollock told people he felt like "a clam without a shell."

Tormented by his inability to work, Pollock became more and more difficult. By the summer of 1956 Lee Krasner could no longer make excuses for his behavior. She announced a trial separation and went to Europe for a few weeks to concentrate on her own painting. While she was gone Pollock, drunk and angry, lost control of his convertible on the country road near their house. Once before he had crashed his car and walked away from the accident. This time he was not so lucky. Jackson Pollock was dead at age forty-four.

To the rest of the world, Jackson Pollock was totally American: violent, unsophisticated, direct. The media had turned him into the myth of the heroic, inarticulate, self-destructive genius, and the way he died confirmed the myth. The paintings he created became the symbols of American artistic liberation.

11

ANDY WARHOL

1928–1987

POP RULES

Andy Warhol's cool, witty images gave us a new way to look at urban life in America, from soup cans to movie stars. Abstract expressionist art had taken itself very seriously. Pop artists moved away from the myth of the abstract expressionist outsider hero toward art for everybody.

Who was Andy Warhol? How did this odd, white-wigged artist who painted soup cans become so famous that when he walked down the street construction workers yelled out, "Hi, Andy"? People are still arguing about the man and his work. He would be pleased. He always said controversy was good for business. There is one thing nobody argues about—Andy Warhol loved publicity, good or bad.

The probable date of Andrew Warhola's birth is August 6, 1928, in Pittsburgh, Pennsylvania. Because his mother, Julia, gave birth to him at home, there was no public record of his birth until 1945, when she gave a signed affidavit of the date so that he could attend college. Warhol said the certificate was a forgery. He claimed to change his birthdate and birthplace at every interview. He said, "I'd prefer to remain a mystery. I never like to give my background and, anyway, I make it all up different every time I'm asked."

His parents had come from Czechoslovakia and settled in Pennsylvania in the early part of the century. Shy, quiet Andy was the youngest of three boys. His mother felt especially protective of him because he was sick as a child. When he was eight years old Andy caught rheumatic fever, a dangerous disease in the days before penicillin was available. He developed a rare complication, chorea, also called Saint Vitus' dance because it causes uncontrolled nervous spasms in the face, arms, and legs.

Chorea is a recurring disease, and several times during his childhood Andy had relapses. He referred to these times as "nervous breakdowns" and wrote almost fondly of sitting in bed with his Charley McCarthy doll beside him, coloring and cutting pictures out of magazines. Every time he finished a page in his coloring book his mother gave him a Hershey bar.

He listened to the family's first radio—recently purchased and placed in his room—and sent away for autographed photographs of movie stars. His favorite was Shirley Temple. He had friends, mostly girls, who shared his devotion to coloring and movie stars, but his brothers described him as a loner who would rather draw than play ball.

Young Andy Warhola.

Andy's father died when Andy was fourteen, leaving money he had carefully saved for his bright youngest son's college tuition. He had told Andy's older brothers to be sure Andy went. In 1945 Andy Warhol was accepted at Carnegie Institute of Technology (now Carnegie Mellon University), a Pittsburgh school near his home with an excellent art department.

Warhol was at a disadvantage in trying to meet the high standards of the college. He was smart enough to have skipped two years in school, but at home his family still spoke mostly Czech. Also, many of the students were veterans returning from World War II; they were more mature and disciplined than recent high-school graduates. At the end of Warhol's freshman year the school decided to drop him.

Several of his teachers went to bat for him, and it was decided to give him another chance. That summer he not only went to special classes at Carnegie Tech and worked at a summer job with his brother, he also car-

THE AMERICAN EYE

ried a sketchbook everywhere. His ability to work hard paid off. The sketchbook full of drawings of his blue-collar neighborhood persuaded the faculty to readmit him that fall. He was given a prize for the best summer work done by a sophomore, and the sketches were exhibited at the school.

Warhol first demonstrated his talent for controversy during his senior year. He submitted a painting to the Associated Artists of Pittsburgh Annual Exhibition, a self-portrait he called *The Broad Gave Me My Face, but I Can Pick My Own Nose*. He was being provocative, but the painting was based on real concerns. To his sorrow, he was not a "beauty." His skin was albino white, except where it was red with acne. He claimed his family called him Andy the red-nosed Warhola because of his large, inflamed nose. Rejected from the show, the painting was the talk of the school. Andy was ready to take on New York.

He prepared a portfolio of his best work and planned to support himself as a commercial artist. He got a freelance job right away, and soon he had others. On the credit line for his first published illustration in *Glamour* magazine "Warhola" was misspelled. Andy always liked the spontaneity of accidents and often incorporated them into his work. He adopted the new spelling—from then on he would be Andy Warhol.

Although he was a prizewinning commercial artist, it wasn't enough. Commercial artists were looked down on by "real" artists, many of whom did commercial art under false names to make a living and used their own names only for their paintings. Warhol wanted to be a "real" artist. He wanted respect.

In 1961 at the Leo Castelli Gallery in New York, he saw something that startled him. He was working on paintings he thought were something new, based on enlargements of comic strips, and now he saw some paintings by another young artist, Roy Lichtenstein, who was doing almost the same thing. Warhol felt he had to find something else.

Warhol dropped the comic-strip paintings, but he was convinced that the common objects that so fascinated him were the right idea. Stuart

FIG. 44 Andy Warhol, *Two Hundred Campbell's Soup Cans,* 1962. Synthetic polymer paint on canvas, 72" × 100".

Davis, another urban artist preoccupied with commercial images, had chosen cigarette packages, spark plug advertisements, and bottles of household cleanser as subjects, but he had flattened the shapes, broken them up, and turned them into paintings.

Warhol's approach was different. He wanted his art to look impersonal and mechanical. To him, the modern way to make art was to follow the path of American industry—mass production, the repetition of the same image over and over again.

He tried rubber stamps, woodcuts, and transfers. Then he started to silk-screen. Sometimes he took a photograph himself; sometimes he blew up an image he wanted to use from a magazine or newspaper. In silk-screening, the image was transferred in glue to a silk screen, and then ink was forced through the screen onto a paper or canvas. Warhol liked mistakes in evenness and registration (the way several ink colors line up) and made them part of the art, so that the pieces were repetitive yet different.

Armed with this new way of working, he went into a creative frenzy. His first inspirations were the Campbell's Soup Can series [FIG. 44], photographs of popular idols like Marilyn Monroe and Elvis Presley, and newspaper photographs of disasters.

Artists such as Georgia O'Keeffe and David Smith had worked in series to explore different aspects of

FIG. 45 Andy Warhol, *Marilyn,* 1986. Acrylic on canvas, 18 1/4" × 14 1/4".

a subject. Warhol's series used repetition in different ways. The same photograph of Marilyn Monroe appeared singly, for example, in black on a silver background, like a movie screen [FIG. 45], and in repeated squares with the color changed in each square.

He also used only the lips from the photograph [FIG. 46], still recognizable as Marilyn's, reproduced in a grid of mouths, reminding us of labels, products, and consumerism. He threw our culture's preoccupations with fame, celebrity, violence, and consumer products in our faces, but not in a holier-than-thou way. Warhol painted what he liked.

These silk screens were shown in an exhibition in November 1962. Faced with something new and startling, people had the usual reaction: They wondered whether the exhibition was a giant joke at their expense.

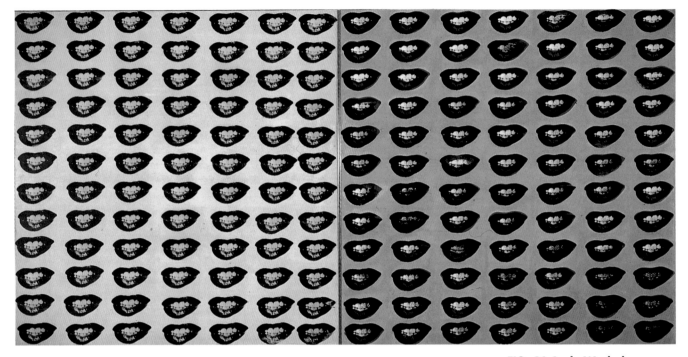

FIG. 46 Andy Warhol,
Marilyn Monroe's Lips, 1962.
Silk-screen ink on synthetic
polymer paint and pencil on
canvas, two panels, 82 1/2″
× 80″ and 83 1/8″ × 83″.

The attitude of the artist only confused them more. Instead of hiding his association with commercial art as other artists did, drawing a dividing line between it and real art, Warhol erased the line.

He said, "The Pop artists did images that anybody walking down Broadway could recognize in a split-second. Comics, picnic tables, men's trousers, celebrities, shower curtains, refrigerators, Coke bottles—all the great modern things that the Abstract Expressionists tried so hard not to notice at all."

About twelve years separated Warhol's *Marilyn Monroe's Lips* from Pollock's *Autumn Rhythm*. In that short time the prevailing fashion in American art had shifted—from passionate abstraction to the impersonal and realistic surface of popular culture. Jackson Pollock had defiantly said, "I am nature." Little more than a decade later Andy Warhol said, "I want to be a machine."

Instead, he became a celebrity. Hip, witty, and open about his homosexuality at a time when most people weren't, he was also unapologetic about his love of movie stars, television, consumerism, and all the things most artists scorned.

In the sixties and seventies the United States rocked with social uproar. Discrimination against minorities and women was challenged in the courts and in the streets. Millions of people marched on Washington in anti–Vietnam War protests. Every traditional authority was questioned.

The public responded to Warhol and his art-is-for-everybody attitude. His shows were a big success. He made large singular works of art, but he also made multiple prints priced so that almost anyone could own one. In addition, he tackled a wide range of subjects, from implied social commentary to portraits of famous people.

Warhol didn't limit himself to painting. He made movies, backed a band called the Velvet Underground (featuring Lou Reed), opened a disco, and started a light show. He became a fixture on the New York social scene, always in the company of young, up-to-the-minute, outrageous people. If he wasn't there, it wasn't a party.

The price of Warhol's fame was high. On June 3, 1968, Valerie Solanis, the founder and sole member of SCUM (Society for Cutting Up Men), shot him. A frustrated screenwriter, she said he had "too much control" over her life. He almost died.

After he was out of the hospital he began publishing *Interview* magazine, wrote several shrewdly amusing books with members of his staff, and started painting again.

Warhol used self-portraits in some of his most provocative works. These two examples, one from 1967, the other from 1986, demonstrate the distance the boy from Pittsburgh had traveled in twenty years, from the shy, rather reflective image to the outrageous Warhol, hair on end, floating on the canvas. In the *Self Portrait* of 1967 [FIG. 47], bubbles of color boil like molten lava out of one side of the head. Accidents are incorporated, making rich textures and giving his silk screen a painterly look. By 1986 the *Self Portrait* [FIG. 48] is flat, graphic, posterlike, and clean on the canvas.

FIG. 47 Andy Warhol, *Self Portrait,* 1967. Silk-screen ink on synthetic polymer paint on canvas, 72″ × 72″.

Warhol feared hospitals and put off operations as long as possible, but in February 1987 doctors warned him he could no longer postpone gall-bladder surgery. He survived the operation, but died that night in the hospital. The last self-portraits, in which his face materialized on the canvas as though from another dimension, had been eerily prophetic.

His death at age fifty-nine was front-page news. Warhol had been the most famous of the pop artists who reacted against the high seriousness of abstract expressionism, and he had made art rooted in the urban American popular culture—democratic art in the most basic sense.

FIG. 48 Andy Warhol, *Self Portrait,* 1986. Silk-screen ink on synthetic polymer paint on canvas, 80″ × 76″.

12

EVA HESSE

1936–1970

THE POWER OF FEMALE IMAGERY

During her short but traumatic life, Eva Hesse opened new frontiers in American art. Like David Smith and many of her contemporaries, she used nonart materials, including latex and fiberglass, to fashion her eccentric, powerful pieces. By combining painted materials with three-dimensional objects, which she hung from the ceiling or wall, Hesse blurred the boundaries between sculpture and painting. Her hands-on approach, which made use of weaving and wrapping, and her sensual forms, which alluded to the human body, gave her pieces a decidedly female quality. Hesse insisted that feminine themes were valid subjects for art.

In high school, Eva Hesse was voted "The Most Beautiful Girl" in her senior class. But in a later self-portrait a different Eva Hesse emerges. Roughly painted in gloomy colors, the picture reveals a hopeless face with one eye punched out; a ghostlike shadow hovers in the background [FIG. 49]. As a woman and artist, Hesse saw herself as haunted and alone. "Art is the easiest thing in my life and that's ironic," she said. "It doesn't mean I've worked little on it, but it's the only thing I never had to. That's why I think I might be so good. I have no fear. I could take risks. . . . I'm willing really to walk on the edge, and if I haven't achieved it, that's where I want to go."

Born into a Jewish family in Germany in 1936, Eva Hesse lived in Hamburg until she was two years old. With the rise of the Nazi Party and increasing anti-Semitism, her parents, fearful for their safety, put Eva and her older sister, Helen, on a train bound for Holland. Their relatives failed to meet them, and the girls were taken to a Catholic children's home. When her mother and father escaped, the family was reunited, but the upheaval of these early years, their flight from Germany to England and finally to the United States, profoundly affected Eva. A fear of abandonment stayed with her all her life.

In New York City, Eva's father, Herman, who had been trained as a criminal lawyer in Germany but was unable to practice in the United States, worked as an insurance broker. Eva's mother, Ruth, whom she

FIG. 49 Eva Hesse, *Self Portrait*, 1961. Oil on canvas, 36″ × 36″.

described as "the most beautiful mother in the world," grew depressed and, after a difficult divorce, took her own life. Eva's father had remarried, and the family lived in an apartment in Washington Heights on Manhattan's West Side. Eva did not get along with her stepmother. At the High School of Industrial Arts, no one noticed Eva's unhappiness because she was a good student who made friends easily. But underneath the veneer of cheerfulness, she felt like a pretender.

"The world thought I was a cute, smart kid, and I kidded them," she said. "But at home I was called a terror. I was miserable. I had . . . incredible fear. I had my father tuck my blankets tight in my German bed which had bars at the bottom, which I would hold at night and he would have to tell me we wouldn't be poor, and we wouldn't be robbed, and he'd be there to take care of me in the morning. As a child it was a ritual every night."

Even as a teenager, Eva Hesse knew she wanted recognition and a career, which was unusual for most young women raised in the 1950s. In a letter to her father she wrote, "Daddy, I want to do more than just exist, to live happily and contented with a home, children, to do the same chores every day."

At sixteen she moved away from home and enrolled in Pratt Institute, a fine-arts college in Brooklyn. In the early 1950s in New York, the reigning style was abstract expressionism, but at Pratt the courses were more traditional. Bored, Hesse waited until she proved to herself she could make A's, and then quit. As soon as she returned home, her stepmother insisted that she get a job.

"So where do you go at sixteen and a half knowing very little but having an interest in art?" Hesse later wrote. "I took myself to *Seventeen* magazine and for some strange reason they hired me."

She worked there part-time and also took classes at the Art Students League. In her free time she went to the Museum of Modern Art and to the movies. The following September she was accepted into Cooper Union, an undergraduate college with a more unstructured art program, which she "loved from the start."

An issue of *Seventeen* from that year included an article about Hesse with color reproductions of some of her watercolors and prints. The interviewer said Hesse felt that "growing up with people who went through the ordeal of those Nazi years makes her look very closely, very seriously under the nature of things." Hesse said, "I paint what I see and feel to express life in all its reality and movement."

Hesse was accepted into Yale Graduate School of Art on a scholarship. "I didn't like [Yale], but because of the combination of being afraid to get out of school—because that was frightening—and not being defeated, I stayed," she said. "In retrospect I don't think I should have stayed. I did well there, but schools depend on both faculty and students and the faculty was poor."

She alternated between intense productivity and periods of frustration, chronicled in diaries that include references to her therapy and her readings in psychology. She was determined to "have a happy love relationship, a family, children," as well as "to fight to be a painter, fight to be healthy. No mediocrity for me."

Hesse moved back to New York in 1960 after finishing graduate school and supported herself by working in a jewelry store. She also immersed herself in the art scene. At the opening of her first group show, she met a charming artist of Irish descent named Tom Doyle, and fell instantly in love. He described their first two years of marriage as "idyllic," but Hesse spoke of competitiveness and the problems of being considered the wife of an artist, rather than being taken seriously as an artist herself. In one of her many notebooks, she expressed a frustration common to many women of her generation. "I cannot be something for everyone. . . . Woman, beautiful, artist, wife, housekeeper, cook, saleslady, all these things. I cannot even be myself, nor know what I am."

People found her charming, talented, and intense, with a childish quality that revealed her vulnerability. Her first one-woman show at New York's Allan Stone Gallery was a series of collages. They indicated a promising talent, but Hesse had yet to come into her own.

An opportunity came along for the couple that was to change the course of her career. Her husband was offered the chance to work for a year in the deserted factory of a German industrialist in exchange for some of his stone sculptures. This was Hesse's first trip to Europe since her childhood escape. Her first weeks in Germany were plagued by nightmares, but gradually she became able to work in the tiny studio constructed for her within the large warehouse space. The use of soft materials, such as rope and papier-mâché, and the grid form, marked the beginnings of her breakthrough work. A small, wide-eyed young woman with long black hair, she posed with her coiled pieces for the catalog of her work done in Germany (see photograph on page 107).

FIG. 50 Eva Hesse, *Hang Up*, 1965–66. Acrylic on cloth over wood and steel, 71" × 77".

Although these pieces demonstrated her new confidence and freedom, she suffered from constant feelings of inadequacy. Hesse was encouraged by her growing friendship with artist Sol LeWitt. He advised her to "stop thinking, worrying, looking over your shoulder, wondering, doubting, fear. . . . Stop it and just DO."

In Germany she experienced the first symptoms of illness, pain in her legs, which was later diagnosed as anemia. At the time she feared her pain was psychosomatic and that, like her mother, she would succumb to mental illness. To add to her anxiety, her marriage was in trouble. She and Tom Doyle began to lead separate lives. When they returned to New York, Doyle eventually left her.

After 1965, Hesse focused all her energies on her work. The German pieces gave her the will to move forward as an artist in her own right. In a piece entitled *Hang Up* [FIG. 50] made shortly after her return from Germany, she constructed a wooden frame that she wrapped in painted rope, out of which projected a steel rod. "It has a kind of depth I don't always achieve—

FIG. 51 Eva Hesse, *Repetition Nineteen, I*, 1967–68. Gouache, watercolor, brush, and pencil on paper, 11 1/4″ × 14 7/8″.

a depth and soul and absurdity . . . or feeling or intellect I want to get."

There is a sense of playfulness and wit in her pieces, "weird humor" as she called it, that relates to her view that life is absurd. The title *Hang Up* itself is a pun—referring to the expression that became popular in the 1960s, as well as to the form of the piece, which "hangs up" on the wall.

In New York, separated from Doyle and living alone, she met a group of artists who rallied around her. For the first time Hesse felt accepted as an artist. It was then that she began to produce an incredible body of work—daring, original pieces such as no one else had done before her. She incorporated weaving, wrapping, sewing, and knitting, traditionally considered women's work, into her pieces. Handcrafting and the use of ordinary materials were very American preoccupations that had roots in early American quilting and weaving.

Toward the end of the 1960s and into the 1970s, the prevailing movement in American sculpture, known as minimalism, used hard materials in geometric shapes. Many of these objects were fabricated in factories. In contrast, Hesse sought to soften her sculpture to show the use of the human hand. There is a fragile, handcrafted quality to *Repetition Nineteen, I* [FIG. 51], but it is made of fiberglass, a product of modern technology. The nineteen hollow buckets, which rest on the floor in random order, are distorted; each is slightly different from the next. One stands upright, and the next seems to be tipping over; another looks as if it might collapse. They remind us of paper bags, dried snakeskins, or human skin. This piece has an appeal like that of odd found objects. The pleasure is in the display, the repetition of forms, the tactile quality of the surface, and the intimacy that the size and placement suggest.

In the following years Hesse achieved the fame and success she so deeply desired. She worked constantly, received critical acclaim, and exhibited her work in galleries and museums. She taught at the School of Visual Arts in New York, traveled, and enjoyed a full social life. Still, she suffered from bouts of depression and loneliness. Increasingly she complained of headaches, dizziness, and vomiting, which doctors diagnosed as depression. Finally in 1969 she was admitted to New York Hospital, where, after many tests, the doctors discovered a brain tumor. She was operated on immediately. As she struggled to recover, she somehow knew that to realize her art in its full capacity, she had to work even harder.

She wrote, "The lack of energy I have is contrasted by a psychic energy of rebirth. A will to start to live again, work again, be seen, love. . . . I'm told and know I must let all those who have asked to help me do so now. It's another new thing to learn."

Although physically weak, she began work on what would become her last major pieces. In *Untitled* [FIG. 52] she coated rope, string, and wire with latex to create a delicate, three-dimensional drawing in space. Suspended from wires in three units, *Untitled* has the spontaneous look of

FIG. 52 Eva Hesse, *Untitled (Rope Piece)*, 1969–70. Latex over rope, string, and wire, two strands, dimensions variable.

a drip painting by Jackson Pollock. The complicated pattern of lines in looping rhythms is unified by Hesse's use of a single color. Here again the notion of weaving and handcrafting comes through. There is a feeling of fragility to the patterns and texture of the piece, a sensuous rhythm, beckoning the viewer into its weblike folds.

By the end of the summer of 1969 Hesse was having headaches again, and a second operation was performed. On May 29, 1970, she died.

A retrospective at the Guggenheim Museum elevated her to martyrlike status. But unlike the stereotype of the tragic heroine driven to madness or suicide, Eva Hesse fought against death and worked right up to the end. Her work has influenced the next generation of artists, especially women, who see the value in using both personal and handcrafted imagery and who share Hesse's belief that an artist's life cannot be separated from her work.

A FINAL NOTE

WHAT NOW?

Although the eleven artists in this book have celebrated and insisted on the Americanness of their art, many have also revealed the conflicts and the dark side of the American dream. Everything we read in the newspapers or see on TV, from international tensions to domestic problems—racism, AIDS, the environment, or crime—finds its way into art. So do the more personal autobiographical concerns—love, joy, and grief. One of the lessons of the twentieth century is that there is no single subject or form of American art; diversity is the key to the American experience.

These days, with global communications, jet travel, and the information superhighway, the world seems smaller. Art has changed, too, and has become more international, less centered on any one country. Artists still dream of making "The Great Painting," but "The Great American Painting" is no longer their goal. No one can predict the future, but one thing is certain—artists will continue to surprise, please, outrage, and challenge us. For the viewer as well as the artist, the goal as we move into the twenty-first century is to continue the dialogue.

Eva Hesse at an exhibition of her work in Germany.

I want to be surprised, to find something new.
I don't want to know the answer before but want
an answer that can surprise.

—Eva Hesse

GLOSSARY

abstract art Art in which the elements of line, shape, texture, or color, rather than a recognizable object, have been stressed.

abstract expressionism A style of art introduced by American artists in the 1940s to express feelings or ideas without a direct reference to subject matter.

aesthetic Concerning the appreciation and perception of the formal and expressive qualities of art.

Ashcan school The name for a group of American artists who painted life in realistic, often urban, aspects, not just "beautiful" and noble subjects.

biomorphic Refers to a shape that looks as if it were reproduced from cells as life is reproduced.

bust A statue of a person's head, neck, and shoulders.

canvas Heavy cotton or linen artists use to paint on. Sometimes it is pulled over a wooden structure called a stretcher, stapled or nailed tightly, and then painted on. Also used as a way of referring to an actual painting: He painted two landscape canvases.

caricature A representation of a person or object in a drawing, painting, or sculpture in which features are exaggerated for humor or satire.

cast A hollow mold from which a work of art can be made. Also the act of making a work of art from a hollow mold by pouring molten metal, liquid plaster, or other material into the mold and letting it harden.

composition The origination of form in a work of art. Also the way the artist chooses to arrange and relate shapes and forms, lines, and colors across the two-dimensional surface of a painting.

cubism An art movement that emerged from Paris in the early 1900s whose chief concern was breaking up the space of a painting by displaying several views of the same object on a single canvas.

dealer A person who sells an artist's work, often at a commercial gallery.

earthworks or earth art Three-dimensional art made of earth, usually noncommercial (not able to be bought or sold), often expressing environmental concerns.

easel A triangular frame of wood or metal that supports a painting while the artist is working on it.

The Eight The name for eight artists who had a group show at the Macbeth Gallery in New York in 1908: Arthur Davies, William Glackens, Robert Henri, Ernest Lawson, George Luks, Maurice Prendergast, Everett Shinn, and John Sloan.

elements The building blocks of art: color, shape, line, and texture.

   color Red, yellow, blue, green, orange, and violet, plus black or white—and all their combinations. Primary colors are red, yellow, and blue.

   shape Refers to the appearance of a particular area in a painting or sculpture, such as a circle or a square.

   line A mark that traces the contours of a form or indicates the direction of the artist's gesture.

      horizontal line A straight line that goes across the canvas, parallel to a horizon or base line.

      vertical line A straight line that goes up and down.

      axis line An imaginary line drawn through shapes and forms to indicate direction in the composition—the thrust, movement, or dynamics of a sculpture or painting.

   texture Refers to the surface of the artwork, especially the way it stimulates our sense of touch.

exhibit A show of artwork, usually in a gallery or museum.

   retrospective exhibit: A show of the work of an artist over a span of time, from early to mature work.

figurative/figural Realistic, or at least recognizable, sculpture or painting of a human subject, a landscape, or an inanimate object. Sometimes used to refer to art that concentrates specifically on the human figure.

form Often used interchangeably with *shape*, but refers specifically to the three-dimensional quality or volume of a shape.

found object An existing nonart object, found or selected and incorporated into a work of art, or displayed for its own aesthetic qualities.

grid A network of evenly spaced squares, flat or three-dimensional, used by many contemporary artists as a system for organizing their images.

impressionism An art movement that emerged from France in the 1870s. Impressionism achieved a new sense of naturalism by exploring light on the surfaces of objects, using dabs of paint in unmixed colors.

landscape A painting in which the land is the subject (though people, animals, or buildings can appear in a landscape).

life A reference to an artist's working from an actual model (not from a photo or a sketch).

medium The material an artist chooses; for example, oil paint, acrylic paint, bronze, or fabric.

minimalism A 1960s art movement emphasizing extreme sparseness and simplicity and relying on simple geometric forms executed in an impersonal style that does not intend to represent any object or emotion beyond itself.

modeling Building up or shaping material such as clay or wax; creating volume with light and shadow. Also, the act of sitting for a painting or sculpture.

monolith A single large block of stone, usually vertical.

old masters A way of referring to the great European painters of the fifteenth, sixteenth, and seventeenth centuries.

organic Having the physical characteristics of living organisms or reminding us of a living form.

painterly A multiuse word that refers to the way a painter puts paint on a surface, usually implying the effect of a brush richly loaded with paint; paint loosely or "brushily" applied. Also loosely contoured forms, rather than hard-edged forms.

palette A piece of material, usually wood or metal, on which the painter lays out his or her colors. Also a way of referring to the colors an artist uses: An artist who uses many bright colors might be said to have a bold palette.

pedestal A structure on which a sculpture stands to set it apart from its surroundings.

pictogram Refers to a symbolic, prehistoric drawing, usually on rock.

pop art An art movement emerging in London and the United States in the 1950s that features images from popular culture—advertising, cartoons, commercial art, and common objects.

portrait A painting usually intended to show what a particular person looked like, but sometimes the artist's impression of the person, rather than a recognizable image.

principles of art Another way of referring to visual effects or balance, emphasis, rhythm, space, unity, and variety.

proportion The relationship and balance of the parts of an artwork to each other and to the work as a whole.

realistic art Sculpture or painting with a recognizable subject that imitates life.

sand painting A method of painting on the earth using various colored sands. Used by Southwestern Native Americans in sacred rituals.

series A group of works by an artist that explores a theme or materials in a variety of ways.

site specific Refers to a work made for a place or "site," usually, though not always, outdoors.

sketch A rough, often preliminary drawing done as a study or outline of an object or scene.

space

    perspective A linear system by which an illusion of depth is achieved on a two-dimensional surface and by which the space is organized from a certain point of view.

    atmospheric perspective The effect of distance in a painting created by using paler or less intense colors to give a faraway effect.

    negative space Empty areas in a painting or sculpture.

    positive space The enclosed area surrounded or defined by negative space.

    figure/ground Another way of talking about positive/negative space.

still life An artwork featuring items arranged by the artist, traditionally depicting domestic and decorative objects, such as bottles, pots, vases, flowers, fruit, and books.

study A drawing, sketch, or roughly finished painting done in preparation for a painting. An artist might do many studies for one painting.

surrealism An art movement that emerged in Paris in the early 1920s, devoted to expressing the unconscious part of the mind through dreamlike, fantastic, or unexpected imagery.

three-dimensional Having, or appearing to have, length, width, and depth.

visual effects The principles of design by which the elements in a sculpture or painting are arranged. Compositional devices, among them balance, emphasis, rhythm, variety, space, and unity.

    formal balance The symmetrical arrangement of the elements of a work of art.

    informal balance The asymmetrical arrangement of the elements of a work of art. The human eye seems to have an inborn ability to tell when something is balanced or in equilibrium; artists often play with this sense.

    emphasis The element that is stressed or most prominent in a work of art.

    rhythm Movement suggested by repeating elements; visual pattern—for example, the repetition of a shape or a color in a work of art to create an effect, or the alternating of a shape with another shape or shapes to the same end.

    variety The many elements or the diversity of one element within a work of art; for example, the use of a number of different shapes or colors to provide contrast and visual interest.

    unity The harmonious or visually satisfying blending of all the visual effects in a work of art.

welding The process of attaching metal parts of a sculpture to each other by melting or brazing with a torch.

LIST OF ARTWORKS

Romare Bearden, *The Afternoon Northbound*, 1978. Mecklenberg County series, collage on board, 15 1/4″ × 20 5/8″. Courtesy estate of Romare Bearden.

Romare Bearden, *The Block,* 1971. Collage of cut and pasted paper and paint on masonite: six panels, 48″ × 216″ overall. Metropolitan Museum of Art, New York. Gift of Mr. and Mrs. Samuel Shore. Courtesy estate of Romare Bearden.

Romare Bearden, *The Street*, 1975. Collage on board, 37 1/2″ × 51″. Courtesy estate of Romare Bearden.

Romare Bearden, *Wrapping It Up at the Lafayette*, 1974. Of the Blues series, collage with acrylic and lacquer on board, 44 1/8″ × 36″. Cleveland Museum of Art. Courtesy estate of Romare Bearden.

Thomas Hart Benton, *The Ballad of the Jealous Lover of Lone Green Valley*, 1934. Egg tempera and oil on canvas, 42 1/2″ × 53 1/4″. Spencer Museum of Art, University of Kansas, Elizabeth M. Watkins Fund. Thomas H. and Rita P. Benton, Benton Testamentary Trusts. VAGA, New York.

Thomas Hart Benton, *Constructivist Still Life*, 1917-18. Oil on cardboard, 12 1/2″ × 8″. 1995 Thomas H. and Rita P. Benton, Benton Testamentary Trusts. VAGA, New York.

Thomas Hart Benton, *Katy Flier, Vinita, Oklahoma*, 1898. Pencil on paper. Private collection. VAGA, New York.

Thomas Hart Benton, *Self-Portrait, South Beach*, 1922. Oil on canvas, 49 1/2″ × 40″. National Portrait Gallery, Smithsonian Institution. Gift of Mr. and Mrs. Jack H. Mooney. 1995 Thomas H. and Rita P. Benton, Benton Testamentary Trusts. VAGA, New York.

Thomas Hart Benton, *Social History of Missouri*, 1935-36 (detail of mural). Missouri Department of Natural Resources, Missouri State Museum. 1995 Estate of Thomas H. and Rita P. Benton, Testamentary Trusts. VAGA, New York.

Stuart Davis, *Egg Beater No. 4*, 1928. Gouache on board, 27″ × 38 1/4″. Phillips Collection, Washington, D.C. 1995 Estate of Earl Davis. VAGA, New York. Photograph courtesy Phillips Collection.

Stuart Davis, *Landscape, Gloucester*, 1922. Oil on canvas, 12″ × 16 1/8″. Private collection, courtesy Borgenicht Gallery, New York. 1995 Estate of Earl Davis. VAGA, New York.

Stuart Davis, *Lucky Strike*, 1924. Oil on paperboard, 18″ × 24″. Hirshhorn Museum and Sculpture Garden, Smithsonian Institution, museum purchase, 1974. Photograph: Lee Stalsworth. 1995 Estate of Earl Davis. VAGA, New York.

Stuart Davis, *Night Life*, 1962. Oil on canvas, 24″ × 32″. Courtesy Greenberg/Van Doren Gallery. 1995 Estate of Earl Davis. VAGA, New York.

Stuart Davis, *Swing Landscape*, 1938. Oil on canvas, 86 3/4″ × 172 1/8″. Indiana University Art Museum. 1995 Estate of Earl Davis. VAGA, New York. Photograph: Michael Cavanagh and Kevin Montague.

Arthur G. Dove, *Abstraction Number 3*, 1910. Oil on composition board. 8 3/8″ × 10 1/2″. Private collection. VAGA, New York.

Arthur G. Dove, *Cow,* 1911. Pastel on linen, 18″ × 20 5/8″. Metropolitan Museum of Art, Alfred Stieglitz Collection, 1949. VAGA, New York.

Arthur G. Dove, *Fog Horns*, 1929. Oil on canvas, 18″ × 26″. Colorado Springs Fine Arts Center. Gift of Oliver B. James. VAGA, New York.

Arthur G. Dove, *Goin' Fishin'*, 1926. Materials on composition board, 19 1/2″ × 24″. Phillips Collection, Washington, D.C. VAGA, New York.

Marcel Duchamp, *Nude Descending a Staircase, No. 2,* 1912. Oil on canvas, 58″ × 35″. Philadelphia Museum of Art, Louise and Walter Arensberg Collection.

Robert Henri, *The Art Student (Portrait of Miss Josephine Nivison),* 1906. Oil on canvas, 77 1/4″ × 38 1/2″. Milwaukee Art Museum. Photograph: Efraim Lever.

Eva Hesse, *Self Portrait,* 1961. Oil on canvas, 36″ × 36″. Collection of Dr. and Mrs. Samuel Dunkell.

Eva Hesse, *Hang Up,* 1965–66. Acrylic on cloth over wood and steel, 71″ × 77″. Art Institute of Chicago, through prior gift of Arthur Keating and Mr. and Mrs. Edward Morris.

Eva Hesse, *Repetition Nineteen, I,* 1967–68. Gouache, watercolor, brush, and pencil on paper, 11 1/4″ × 14 7/8″. Museum of Modern Art, New York. Gift of the Eva Hesse Estate. Photograph © 1994 The Museum of Modern Art.

Eva Hesse, *Untitled (Rope Piece),* 1969–70. Latex over rope, string, and wire, two strands, dimensions variable. Whitney Museum of American Art, purchased with funds from Eli and Edythe L. Broad, the Mrs. Percy Uris Purchase Fund, and the Painting and Sculpture Committee. Photograph: Geoffrey Clements.

Edward Hopper, *Chop Suey,* 1929. Oil on canvas, 32″ × 38″. Collection of Mr. and Mrs. Barney A. Ebsworth.

Edward Hopper, jacket illustration for *Hotel Management,* January 1925.

Edward Hopper, *House by the Railroad,* 1925. Oil on canvas, 24″ × 29″. Museum of Modern Art, New York. Given anonymously. Photograph © 1994 The Museum of Modern Art.

Edward Hopper, *Second Story Sunlight,* 1960. Oil on canvas, 40″ × 50″. Collection of the Whitney Museum of American Art, New York, purchased with funds from the Friends of the Whitney Museum of American Art. Photograph: Geoffrey Clements.

Edward Hopper, *Western Motel,* 1957. Oil on canvas, 24″ × 29″. Yale University Art Gallery. Bequest of Stephen Carlton Clark, B.A. 1903.

Isamu Noguchi, *Ikiru (To Live),* 1952. Concrete bridge railing, Two Bridges for Peace Park, Hiroshima, Japan. Courtesy of the Isamu Noguchi Foundation.

Isamu Noguchi, *Humpty Dumpty,* 1946. Ribbon slate, 58 3/4″ high. Collection of the Whitney Museum of American Art, New York. Photograph: Jerry L. Thompson.

Isamu Noguchi, *Jardin Japonais,* 1956–58. UNESCO Headquarters, Paris. Photograph: Isamu Noguchi. Courtesy of the Isamu Noguchi Foundation.

Isamu Noguchi, *The Stone Within,* 1982. Basalt, 75″ high. Isamu Noguchi Garden Museum. Photograph: Michio Noguchi. Courtesy of the Isamu Noguchi Foundation.

Georgia O'Keeffe, *Special No. 9,* 1915. Charcoal on paper, 25″ × 19 1/8″. Menil Collection, Houston. Photograph: Malcolm Varon. ARS, New York.

Georgia O'Keeffe, *Music Pink and Blue I,* 1919. Oil on canvas, 35″ × 29″. Collection of Mr. and Mrs. Barney A. Ebsworth. ARS, New York.

Georgia O'Keeffe, *Calla Lily,* 1930. Oil on board, 6″ × 4 2/3″. Collection of Mr. and Mrs. Marvin Moskowitz. ARS, New York.

Georgia O'Keeffe, *Cow's Skull: Red, White, and Blue,* 1931. Oil on canvas, 39 7/8″ × 35 7/8″. Metropolitan Museum of Art, Alfred Stieglitz Collection, 1952. ARS, New York.

Pablo Picasso, *Glass and Bottle of Bass,* 1914. Charcoal, pencil, india ink, white gouache, newspaper, and woodblock-printed papers pasted on wood pulp board, 20 5/16″ × 26 11/16″. Private collection. Photograph: Bob Kolbrener. ARS, New York.

Jackson Pollock, *Going West,* 1934–35. Oil on fiberboard, 15 1/8″ × 20 1/4″. National Museum of American Art, Smithsonian Institution. Gift of Thomas Hart Benton. ARS, New York.

Jackson Pollock, *Guardians of the Secret,* 1943. Oil on canvas, 48 3/8″ × 75 3/8″. San Francisco Museum of Modern Art, Albert M. Bender Collection. Albert M. Bender Bequest Fund Purchase. Photograph: Don Myer. ARS, New York.

Jackson Pollock, *Full Fathom Five,* 1947. Oil on canvas with nails, tacks, buttons, key, coins, cigarettes, matches, etc., 50 7/8″ × 30 1/8″. Museum of Modern Art, New York. Gift of Peggy Guggenheim. Photograph © 1994 The Museum of Modern Art. ARS, New York.

Jackson Pollock, *Number 1, 1948,* 1948. Oil and enamel on unprimed canvas, 68″ × 104″. Museum of Modern Art, New York. Purchase. Photograph © 1994 The Museum of Modern Art. ARS, New York.

David Smith, *Construction,* 1932. Wood, wire, nails, and coral, painted red, blue, and yellow, 37 1/8″ × 16 1/4″ × 7 1/4″. 1995 Estate of David Smith. VAGA, New York.

David Smith, *Cubi IX,* 1961. Stainless steel, 105 3/4″ × 58 5/8″ × 43 7/8″. Walker Art Center, Minneapolis. Gift of the T. B. Walker Foundation. VAGA, New York.

David Smith, *Voltron XX,* 1963. Steel, 62 1/4″ ·× 37 1/2″ × 26 1/2″. Storm King Art Center, Mountainville, New York. Gift of the Ralph E. Ogden Foundation. Photograph: Jerry L. Thompson. VAGA, New York.

Alfred Stieglitz, *The Street, Winter,* 1903. Gelatin silver print. Metropolitan Museum of Art. Gift of J. B. Neumann, 1958.

Andy Warhol, *Marilyn,* 1986. Acrylic on canvas, 18 1/4″ × 14 1/4″. Private collection. ARS, New York.

Andy Warhol, *Marilyn Monroe's Lips,* 1962. Silk- screen ink on synthetic polymer paint and pencil on canvas, two panels, 82 1/2″ × 80″ and 83 1/8″ × 83″. Hirshhorn Museum and Sculpture Garden, Smithsonian Institution, Washington, D.C. Gift of Joseph H. Hirshhorn. Photograph: Lee Stalsworth. ARS, New York.

Andy Warhol, *Two Hundred Campbell's Soup Cans,* 1962. Synthetic polymer paint on canvas, 72″ × 100″. Collection of John and Kimiko Powers. ARS, New York.

Andy Warhol, *Self Portrait,* 1967. Silk-screen ink on synthetic polymer paint on canvas, 72″ × 72″. Private collection. ARS, New York.

Andy Warhol, *Self Portrait,* 1986. Silk-screen ink on synthetic polymer paint on canvas, 80″ × 76″. Private collection. ARS, New York.

WHERE TO FIND WORKS BY THE ARTISTS IN THIS BOOK

Large and small museums across the United States own works by the artists in this book. Listed below are a few places where these works can be viewed.

Romare Bearden: Metropolitan Museum of Art, New York. Schomburg Center for Research in Black Culture, New York Public Library. Mint Museum, Charlotte, North Carolina. Cleveland Museum of Art, Ohio. Asheville Art Museum, North Carolina.

Thomas Hart Benton: Kemper Museum, Kansas City Art Institute, Missouri. Metropolitan Museum of Art, New York. Thomas Hart Benton House, Kansas City, Missouri. (The house Benton lived in has been turned into a museum and study center.) State Capitol Building, Jefferson City, Missouri. (There are murals throughout the building.)

Stuart Davis: Hirshhorn Museum and Sculpture Garden, Smithsonian Institution, Washington, D.C. Indiana University Art Museum, Bloomington. Museum of Fine Art, Houston. Los Angeles County Museum of Art. Brooklyn Museum, New York.

Arthur Dove: Phillips Collection, Washington, D.C. (The founder of this museum was Dove's patron, Duncan Phillips.) Metropolitan Museum of Art, New York. Museum of Fine Arts, Boston.

Eva Hesse: Allen Memorial Art Museum, Oberlin College, Ohio. Museum of Modern Art, New York. Wadsworth Atheneum, Hartford, Connecticut. Detroit Institute of Fine Arts.

Edward Hopper: Whitney Museum of American Art, New York. Hopper House, Nyack, New York. (Hopper's boyhood home is now a museum containing prints and memorabilia.) National Museum of American Art, Smithsonian Institution, Washington, D.C.

Isamu Noguchi: Isamu Noguchi Garden Museum, Long Island City, New York. (The building where Noguchi lived and worked in New York is now a museum containing many of his works.) South Coast Plaza, Costa Mesa, California. (This is a sculpture garden designed and created by Noguchi.) Horace E. Dodge Fountain, 1972–79, Philip A. Hart Plaza, Detroit.

Georgia O'Keeffe: Art Institute of Chicago. Carl van Vechten Gallery of Fine Arts at Fisk University, Nashville. Amon Carter Museum, Fort Worth. National Gallery of Art, Smithsonian Institution, Washington, D.C.

Jackson Pollock: Pollock-Krasner House, Springs, New York. (The house and studio in Springs are now a museum and study center; by appointment.) Museum of Modern Art, New York. Menil Collection, Houston.

David Smith: National Gallery of Art, Smithsonian Institution, Washington, D.C. Storm King Sculpture Center, Mountainville, New York. St. Louis Art Museum, Missouri.

Andy Warhol: Albright-Knox Art Gallery, Buffalo. Andy Warhol Museum, Pittsburgh. (This is a new museum containing only works by Warhol.) Virginia Museum of Fine Arts, Richmond. Baltimore Museum of Art, Maryland.

BIBLIOGRAPHY

GENERAL

Hunter, Sam. *American Art of the 20th Century*. New York: Harry N. Abrams, 1972.

Kuh, Katherine. *The Artist's Voice: Talks with Seventeen Artists*. New York: Harper & Row, 1962.

O'Doherty, Brian. *American Masters, The Voice and the Myth*. With photographs by Hans Namuth. New York: Universe Books, 1988.

Rose, Barbara. *American Painting: Twentieth Century*. New York: Rizzoli International Publications, 1969.

Russell, John. *The Meaning of Modern Art*. New York: Harper & Row, 1981.

ARTHUR DOVE

Haskell, Barbara. *Arthur Dove*. Boston: New York Graphic Society, 1974.

Morgan, Ann Lee. *Arthur Dove: Life and Work*. Newark: University of Delaware Press, 1984.

———, ed. *Dear Stieglitz, Dear Dove*. London: Association of University Presses, 1988.

Wight, Frederick S. *Arthur Garfield Dove*. Berkeley and Los Angeles: University of California Press, 1958.

GEORGIA O'KEEFFE

Cowart, Jack, and Hamilton, Juan. *Georgia O'Keeffe: Art and Letters*, selected and annotated by Sarah Greenough. Boston: Little, Brown, 1987.

Giboire, Clive, ed. *Lovingly, Georgia: The Complete Correspondence of Georgia O'Keeffe and Anita Pollitzer*. New York: Simon & Schuster/Touchstone, 1990.

O'Keeffe, Georgia. *Georgia O'Keeffe*. New York: Viking, 1976.

Pollitzer, Anita. *A Woman on Paper: Georgia O'Keeffe, The Letters and Memoir of a Legendary Friendship*. New York: Touchstone, 1968.

Robinson, Roxana. *Georgia O'Keeffe*. New York: HarperCollins, 1989.

EDWARD HOPPER

Catalog: Edward Hopper, Light Years. Essay by Peter Schjeldahl. New York: Hirschl & Adler Galleries, Inc.

Goodrich, Lloyd. *Edward Hopper*. New York: Harry N. Abrams, 1983.

Hobbs, Robert. *Edward Hopper*. New York: Harry N. Abrams in association with the National Museum of American Art, 1987.

Levin, Gail. *Edward Hopper: The Art and the Artist*. New York: W. W. Norton in association with the Whitney Museum of American Art, 1980.

———. *Edward Hopper as Illustrator*. New York: W. W. Norton in association with the Whitney Museum of American Art, 1979.

THOMAS HART BENTON

Adams, Henry. *Thomas Hart Benton: An American Original*. New York: Alfred A. Knopf, 1989.

Benton, Thomas Hart. *An Artist in America*. Columbia: University of Missouri Press, 1937.

———. *An American in Art*. Lawrence: University Press of Kansas, 1969.

Yeo, Wilma, and Cook, Helen. *Maverick with a Paintbrush: Thomas Hart Benton*. Garden City, New York: Doubleday, 1977.

STUART DAVIS

Blesh, Rudi. *Stuart Davis*. New York: Grove Press, 1960.

Kelder, Diane, ed. *Stuart Davis*. New York: Praeger, 1971.

Myers, Jane, ed. *Stuart Davis: Graphic Work and Related Paintings.* Catalogue Raisonée of the Prints. Fort Worth: Amon Carter Museum, 1986.

Stuart Davis Memorial Exhibition 1894–1964. National Collection of Fine Art. Washington, D.C.: Smithsonian Institution, 1965.

Stuart Davis. Excerpted from American Artists Group, Inc., Monograph No. 6, 1945, pp. 1–10.

Sweeney, James Johnson. *Stuart Davis.* New York: Museum of Modern Art, 1945.

ROMARE BEARDEN
Campbell, Mary Schmidt, and Patton, F. Sharon. *Memory and Metaphor: The Art of Romare Bearden, 1940–1987.* New York: Oxford University Press, 1991.

Schwartzman, Myron. *Romare Bearden: His Life and Art.* New York: Harry N. Abrams, 1990.

Washington, M. Bunch. *The Art of Romare Bearden: The Prevalence of Ritual.* New York: Harry N. Abrams, 1973.

ISAMU NOGUCHI
Altshuler, Bruce. *Noguchi.* New York, London, and Paris: Abbeville Press, 1994.

Ashton, Dore. *Noguchi East and West.* New York: Alfred A. Knopf, 1992.

Hau, Amy. Interview with the authors, Isamu Noguchi Garden Museum, Long Island City, New York, 1983.

Noguchi, Isamu. *A Sculptor's World.* New York: Harper & Row, 1968.

———. *The Isamu Noguchi Garden Museum.* New York: Harry N. Abrams, 1987.

DAVID SMITH
Carnean, E. A., Jr. *David Smith.* Washington, D.C.: National Gallery of Art, 1982.

Gray, Cleve, ed. *David Smith: Sculpture and Writings by David Smith.* London: Thames & Hudson, 1968.

Wilkin, Karen. *David Smith.* New York: Abbeville Press, 1984.

JACKSON POLLOCK
Frank, Elizabeth. *Pollock.* New York, London and Paris: Abbeville Press, 1983.

Landau, Ellen G. *Jackson Pollock.* New York: Harry N. Abrams, 1989.

Naifeh, Steven, and Smith, Gregory White. *Jackson Pollock: An American Saga.* New York: Clarkson N. Potter, 1989.

Potter, Jeffrey. *To a Violent Grave: An Oral Biography of Jackson Pollock.* New York: G. P. Putnam, 1985.

ANDY WARHOL
Bockris, Victor. *The Life and Death of Andy Warhol.* New York: Bantam, 1989.

McShine, Kynaston, ed. *Catalog. Andy Warhol: A Retrospective.* With essays by Kynaston McShine, Robert Rosenblum, Benjamin H. D. Buchloh, Marco Livingston. New York: Museum of Modern Art, 1989.

Ratcliff, Carter. *Warhol.* New York: Abbeville Press, 1983.

Smith, Patrick S. *Warhol: Conversations About the Artist.* Ann Arbor, Michigan: UMI Research Press, 1988.

EVA HESSE
Cooper, Helen. *Eva Hesse: A Retrospective.* New Haven: Yale University Art Library, 1992.

Lippard, Lucy R. *Eva Hesse.* New York: New York University Press, 1976.

Nemser, Cindy. *Arttalk: Conversations with Twelve Women Artists.* New York: Charles Scribner's Sons, 1975.

INDEX

ABOUT THE AUTHORS

Jan Greenberg is a writer, teacher, and art educator who directed the Aesthetic Education Master of Arts in Teaching program at Webster University in St. Louis. She is also the author of a number of award-winning books for young readers. She lives in St. Louis.

Sandra Jordan is a writer and photographer. For many years she was an editor of books for young readers. She and Jan Greenberg are the coauthors of *The Painter's Eye: Learning to Look at Contemporary American Art* and *The Sculptor's Eye: Looking at Contemporary American Art.* She grew up in Cleveland and lives in New York City.